Jennifer Leach was born and raised in Leeds and has always had an urge to write books but just never had the time or the chance. At the age of twenty-seven, while suffering with a chest infection, she took the opportunity to write her first book *Royal Blood – The Knights*.

To L. J Smith, my favourite author. Thank you for being such an amazing writer. Truly an inspiration to myself and others.

Jennifer Leach

ROYAL BLOOD – THE KNIGHTS

AUSTIN MACAULEY PUBLISHERS™
LONDON • CAMBRIDGE • NEW YORK • SHARJAH

Copyright © Jennifer Leach 2022

The right of Jennifer Leach to be identified as author of this work has been asserted by the author in accordance with section 77 and 78 of the Copyright, Designs and Patents Act 1988.

All rights reserved. No part of this publication may be reproduced, stored in a retrieval system, or transmitted in any form or by any means, electronic, mechanical, photocopying, recording, or otherwise, without the prior permission of the publishers.

Any person who commits any unauthorised act in relation to this publication may be liable to criminal prosecution and civil claims for damages.

This is a work of fiction. Names, characters, businesses, places, events, locales, and incidents are either the products of the author's imagination or used in a fictitious manner. Any resemblance to actual persons, living or dead, or actual events is purely coincidental.

A CIP catalogue record for this title is available from the British Library.

ISBN 9781398417120 (Paperback)
ISBN 9781398417137 (ePub e-book)

www.austinmacauley.com

First Published 2022
Austin Macauley Publishers Ltd®
1 Canada Square
Canary Wharf
London
E14 5AA

A massive thank you to Austin Macauley Publishers for giving me the opportunity to publish my work and making a long-time dream come true.

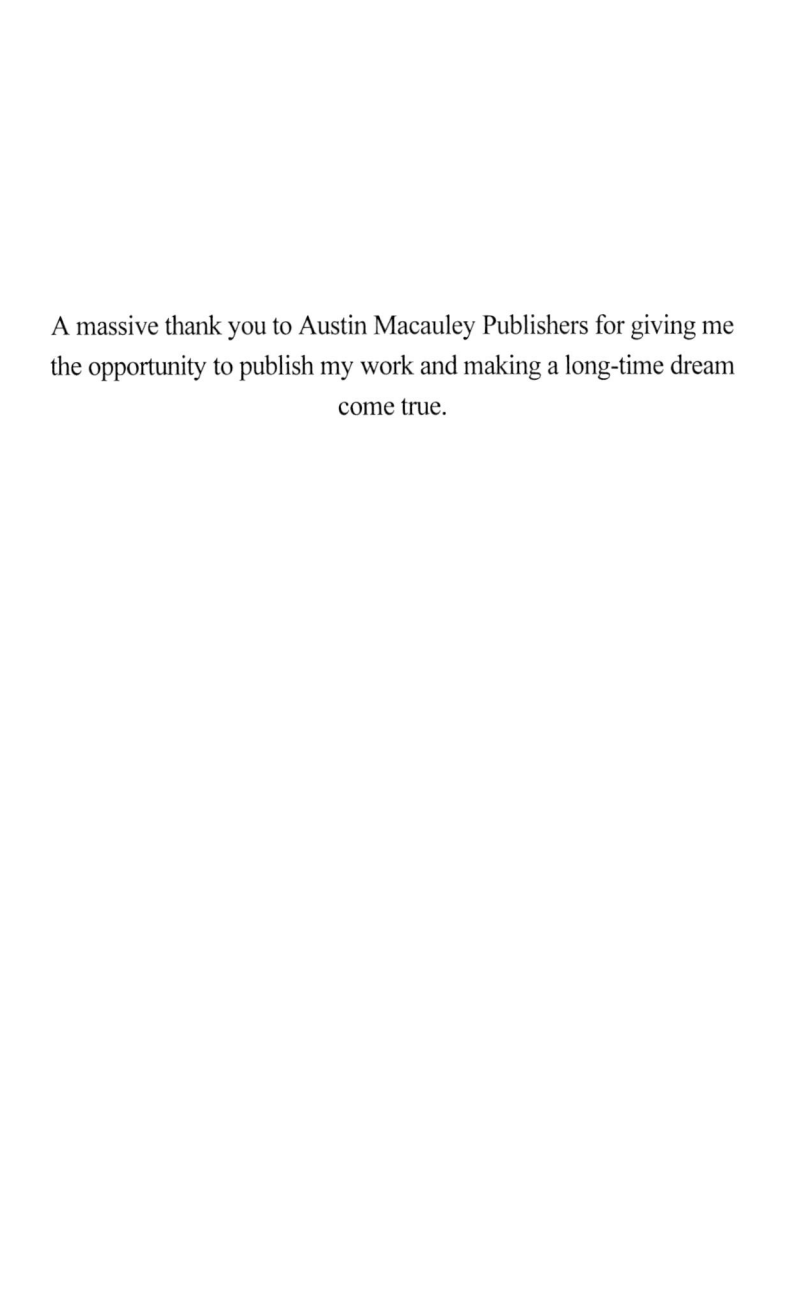

Prologue

The young girl was tossed to the floor like an unwanted ragdoll. Her clover green eyes, once full of life, were now empty. Her rose pink lips were now a mixture of blue and purple. The pair of puncture marks on her neck was deep, red, and angry.

Wiping his mouth with the back of his hand, James never took his eyes off the dead girl who lay lifeless at his feet. Closing his eyes, James ran his tongue over his teeth to remove the remnants. At the same time, savouring the taste of the warm coppery fluid. The blood coursed through his veins with a rush; it had been a *very* long time since he had felt this excited.

Standing tall, James's body glowed silver with revival in the moonlight. Kicking the girl out of his path, smirking as her bones cracked, he walked towards the window. Solemnly, his sharp emerald eyes just stared up into the navy night sky. The moon was full and ripe tonight.

Chapter One

"Charlotte!" Vicky Reed shouted as she wrestled her mousy brown hair into a ponytail. "Hurry up!"

Charlotte Davenport, second-year English Literature student, smiled with amusement at her own reflection in the mirror, as she brushed her mahogany brown hair. "Coming!"

Vicky popped her head into the doorway, staring with fake seriousness at her best friend and housemate. "If we're late," she said, "I'm blaming you." Charlotte just continued to brush her hair, still smiling. Vicky then stood fully in the doorway; folding her arms, her hazel eyes observed Charlotte more closely. Pencil skirt and tight-fit jumper? "You're looking very pretty today."

"Do I?"

Vicky nodded slowly, then shrugged it off and went back into the hallway. "I'm going to start the car. See you in a minute."

"In a minute." Charlotte responded while checking her makeup. Satisfied with the result, she let her dark chocolate eyes skim over the clothes chosen for today. A black pencil skirt with a high-necked cream jumper that clung tightly to her waist. Not normally the usual college attire, but today was a different day. Although, she didn't quite know why. A tiny bit of lipstick, Charlotte thought to herself, and done. Charlotte didn't wear a lot of makeup. With thick dark hair and dark eyes to match, beige creamy skin, she didn't need it, yet she still turned a few heads.

Nodding with approval, Charlotte put her lipstick away in her bag and headed into the hallway and towards the front door. Handbag in hand, she opened the door and stepped out into a grey dreary morning, the usual sky blue Vauxhall Corsa waited at the edge of the curb, a very impatient Vicky Reed tapping at the wheel. After locking the front door, Charlotte opened the car door, threw her bag into the back and got settled into the passenger seat.

"Ready?" Vicky asked.

Charlotte smiled innocently at her friend. "Whenever you are."

Vicky scoffed and shook her head; turning the key, the engine came to life and Vicky drove the car out of Salisbury Grove and onto the main road. "Blaming you," she muttered.

"For what?"

"If we're late again! You do realise it is a Friday night and I would like to be home at a reasonable hour today without a lecture."

"Like that will ever happen," Charlotte muttered.

"True," Vicky replied, checking both left and right, before pulling out. As the car pulled onto the main road, up ahead, you could already see the tall silver office buildings of Leeds City Centre.

Nicholas Rinaldi stared down at the blonde-haired girl, who laid so still and calm beneath him on the bed. Rose Calvert's large hazel eyes, which were a perfect mix of green and brown, glittered up at him with adoration. Her rose pink lips curled at the ends in a small, loving, satisfied smile. Behind it, her own teeth had lengthened slightly with excitement. Her thick wavy locks were sprayed over the bed sheets like water. The two marks on her neck were red and fresh.

Nicholas was still tense, his muscles were hard and could be seen through his black turtleneck jumper. His pair of canines long and poised, was stained with Rose's blood. Nicholas lifted a large hand from the side of Rose's head, and used the back of it to wipe his mouth, never once blinking or taking his eyes away from the beauty beneath him. Rose had been coming to his room more often these days, willingly offering herself, without expecting anything in return. Although, Nicholas and everybody else knew what she wanted. It was the same routine, Rose would enter his room, have some small conversation, lay on the bed and Nicholas would take what he wanted. Even though they both knew he didn't need it. Nicholas Rinaldi was a rare breed of his kind; unlike so many, he did not need to feed on a regular basis. *That* made him a royal.

Sensing his muscles calm and relax, Nicholas lifted himself off Rose and sat on the edge of the bed. His canines began to return to their normal state. It wasn't long after that Rose joined him. Kneeling on the bed, she put a slender hand on his shoulder, her head tilted in concern. "My Lord?" Her voice was so soft.

A few moments went by, of just staring at the wall opposite, before Nicholas reached over and took her hand in his. Kissing the back of it, he reassured her. "I'm alright." Another moment seemed to pass between them before he spoke again softly. "You'd better go and get ready."

Without question, Rose nodded and accepted the hand Nicholas offered to assist her off the bed. Adjusting her tight-fit dress, she walked straight for the bedroom door, just simply opening it, and closing it behind her. Nicholas just continued to stare.

Walking down the stairs onto the landing, Rose lightly touched the marks on her slender neck. Her body's healing process had begun, and in no time at all, the skin had returned to its more suitable state. When Rose got to the edge of the stairs, she was stopped dead by a pair of dangerous brown eyes.

Dominic McKnight was leaning casually against the wall, his arms and legs crossed and his god-like features, stern. His lips were slightly twisted in disgust as he stared at the female before him. "You did it again, didn't you?" It was more of a statement than a question. When Rose didn't answer, Dominic asked again. "Didn't you?"

Silence passed between the pair before Rose, more or less, sneered at Dominic. Folding her arms, she growled. "So what?" Rose's face became a scowl, like a cat on the defence. "What's it got to do with you? It's my decision what I do with *my* life, *my* body, *my* bl—"

"But that's just it. Have you no pride?" Dominic interrupted softly, but sternly. The words caught Rose off-guard, her mouth fell agape, slightly. Dominic just shook his head in despair. "Why are you doing this to yourself?"

Rose just stared blankly at him. "Because I have no one else."

Dominic recalled that Rose was the daughter of a very ambitious family. Clearly, the girl had been given instructions. But this was no excuse. "What do you think is going to happen at the end of the year? You think he's going to scoop you up into his arms? Choose you above everyone else to be by his side? Even if he could, his father would never allow you to enter their circle." Dominic paused to let his words sink in. "Nicholas is a royal. His purpose in life has already been decided. His life is more or less laid out. No matter what your family wants you to do, the plan for Nicholas, does *not* include *you*." Rose's face remained emotionless. Dominic in a small way, pitied her. Sighing, he turned his back and headed down the second set of stairs. "Clean yourself up. Bianca and Edward are waiting."

Chapter Two

The classroom was already echoing with the voices of the other English Literature students. As usual, the Friday night ahead was causing a wave of excitement throughout the college. Both Charlotte and Vicky emptied their books and notepads onto their desks and casually took a seat. For once, it was their tutor who was late.

"Have you decided what you're doing yet?" Vicky asked while adjusting her ponytail.

"Probably just move back home with Uncle Carl for a bit," Charlotte replied. "Get a job back home and go from there. You?"

"I've decided I'm not moving back in. I think I'd actually enjoy just being by myself for a bit."

"Would you stay in the house we're in now?" Charlotte asked curiously. "Or find somewhere else?"

"Definitely find somewhere else," Vicky replied without hesitation. "I want a nice apartment near the river."

Charlotte rolled her eyes. "You would."

Vicky just smiled in her friend's direction. "Is your uncle still coming around tomorrow?"

"I think so. He hasn't said otherwise. Wants to take me out for lunch."

Vicky just grinned as the class suddenly became a room of more excitable yet quieter whispers and giggles. It didn't take very long to realise why. "Here we go," Vicky muttered in Charlotte's direction who just responded with a sideways glance, before turning her attention back to the doorway. Of course, Stephanie Ross, an auburn-haired girl, began checking her makeup and quickly rearranging her hair.

Stepping into the class, the five most popular people in the college walked in. It was the same every day; as soon as the door opened, the class and the entire college in fact, became like a hive of bees, just buzzing with gossip. As usual, Edward Blake and Bianca DeLuca walked in side by side. Edward was a tall, broad shouldered boy with a young boyish face. However, his facial features were sharp and cunning like a fox. His hair was a thick, reddish brown and his eyes were a strange seaweed green. Next to him, his girlfriend and fashion trendsetter; Bianca who compared to Edward, was tiny. Bianca's hair was pixie-cut and fiery ginger, and her eyes were a pair of rare sapphires that were cold and dangerous. Then came Rose Calvert, the envy of most young girls. An ivory-skinned girl with thick, wavy blonde hair with the most exquisite hazel eyes. Dominic McKnight was the largest out of all of them. Broad shouldered, muscular, tall, dark-haired, dark-eyed. His colouring was very similar to Charlotte's, but only a shade lighter. Lastly, Nicholas Rinaldi. Always smartly dressed and walked with both, a sense of pride and authority. Compared to the other two boys in his group, Nicholas was of medium height, jet-black hair and jet-black eyes. Like Dominic, he was also broad-shouldered, only not as muscular.

Charlotte couldn't help but frown at Nicholas as he strode into class; he was the only one that she truly felt a tad curious about. But for some reason, always got a sense of danger around him. An inner thought always begged her to stay away. Charlotte remembered their early days in high school. From day one, they never got on. Nicholas always treated Charlotte with a feeling of contempt, as though she had offended him in some way. Not with words, but with cold looks and ignorance. Every time they passed through a corridor, Charlotte felt Nicholas's deadly eyes burning into her back, as though he urged her to set alight. *Danger.* Yet by the end of high school, Nicholas seemed to change. To Charlotte's surprise, Nicholas started to acknowledge her with small nods, small talk, even asking about her family. Of course, much to the annoyance of the other girls, especially Stephanie, who were desperate to catch his eye. Other than curiosity, Charlotte was probably the only one who had no interest in Nicholas whatsoever.

As Nicholas took his seat with the rest of his circle at the back of the class, he immediately sensed a pair of eyes on him. Looking up, Charlotte was staring with her usual curious frown. Smiling politely, Nicholas nodded in her direction. "Morning."

"Morning," she quickly muttered back.

Not long after the five of them had taken their seats, the English Literature tutor rushed into the class. Dumping her books onto the desk, she ushered the rest of the students to take their seats, then adjusting her glasses, she addressed the class with a sense of seriousness in her voice. "Good morning, everyone." She paused to give the class time to respond. "I'm afraid I have to start today with some very sad news. As you are all aware, there have been some disappearances of young girls from our college." The tutor paused once again to clear her throat. "I'm sorry to say that Samantha has been found."

Like a beehive, the class buzzed in ecstatic conversation. Voices of shock and panic echoed throughout the room. Charlotte already managed to pick up a few words from the students in front of her.

"Sam…?"

"Dead…?"

"Throat ripped open…?"

"Broke…"

"We were out…"

The tutor tried to calm the class by demanding silence but it was near enough impossible; shock had already set in. Charlotte and Vicky could do nothing but look at each other with the same expression of worry and concern. At the back of the class, Nicholas, Rose, Dominic, Bianca and Edward all shared a sideways glance to each other. This was this third girl to go missing within the month, in the same area.

Chapter Three

The lunchtime bell rang and the canteen soon flooded with students. Charlotte took a bite out of the sandwich she had purchased while Vicky went on to read the article in her hands. Newspapers were laid out on all the tables, with Samantha Collins as the front-page news.

"Samantha Collins," Vicky read aloud. "Aged twenty, has been missing since 12 August. She was last seen out with friends in Leeds City Centre. Police say they have found a body that has been positively identified as Samantha Collins." Vicky paused before reading it aloud. "Miss Collins was found with the same stab wounds to her neck as the other victims. However, Miss Collins was also found with her back snapped in half, unlike the other two victims."

"Oh God," Charlotte muttered quietly.

Vicky put down the paper and took to making a start on her own lunch. "Police are telling everyone to be careful. All young girls should walk home in groups instead of pairs."

"They will do," Charlotte replied. "With a serial killer on the loose…" Her lips thinned sadly as she thought *Poor Sam.*

"I know," Vicky agreed quietly. "She was nice. Why would someone do this? To Sam of *all* people; she never did anything to anyone."

Charlotte nodded in agreement as she picked up the paper to look at the picture of Samantha Collins. The picture showed Sam with her family who looked as though they were on some sort of fishing trip. Charlotte smiled sadly at the photograph. Sam looked so happy and pretty. With a smile that could light up a room, she could cheer anyone up on their darkest day. Admittedly, Charlotte didn't really have anything to do with Sam while she was alive. But when they did speak, Sam always came across as cheerful and polite. Letting out a little sad sigh, Charlotte put the paper down and got back to finishing her lunch.

To change the subject, Vicky chirped up. "Did I hear" – she paused cunningly – "Nicholas say morning to you today?"

"Yep." Charlotte replied, not even looking at Vicky.

"And?"

"And…what?"

"Oh, come on," Vicky chirped once again. Her trademark smirk not leaving her face. "That's more attention than what anyone else gets."

"So?"

"*So*, considering you two didn't really get on at first, I'd say you've come along way. And Nicholas does single you out from everyone else. Have you noticed that he's only ever gone around with Rose, Edward, Bianca and Dominic, for as long as we've known him? And yet, he talks to *you*."

Charlotte folded her arms across the table, and shrugged. "I don't care."

"He's rich."

"I don't care."

"I bet he's got some nice cars."

"Don't care."

"Nice house?" Vicky's smirked broadened cunningly. "I bet he's good in bed."

Charlotte's mouth opened slightly in astonishment. "I am now terminating this conversation." She said as she picked up her sandwich.

Vicky just laughed.

Nicholas kneeled down by the water, intently watching it as it flowed and swirled flawlessly and gently. Reaching out a hand, he dipped the tips of his fingers into the cold water; trying to find a sign or a scent of *anything*. The hour lunch break could not have come quick enough for him. Closing his eyes, taking in a nice calm breath, Nicholas focused.

Bianca, Rose, Edward and Dominic were spread out across the area, also searching for signs of any creature daring enough to do this. But Nicholas was positive that they wouldn't find anything. Here, there was no sound. No birds, no crickets, just the soft sound of running water and the breeze. *Why here? All the girls were attacked in areas so close to each other. Why hasn't it moved on to avoid being discovered? What is it looking for?* Nicholas thought to himself. All three girls were similar ages, all were blonde, and green-eyed, all from the same college. Nicholas slowly opened his eyes at a sudden thought; *all* blonde, *all* green-eyed. Nicholas stared down into the water's edge where his fingertips were. His keen eyesight staring intently at his reflection in the water as he stood up straight. "Mother."

"My Lord."

Nicholas turned his head slightly to look over his shoulder at Bianca and Edward. "Anything?"

"Nothing," Edward replied. "We checked the park, the edge of the town, the bridges. There's no sign that this was one of our own."

Nicholas sneered. "You think this was done by a human? Or an animal?"

"That's not what I meant," Edward said bluntly, earning a raised eyebrow from both Bianca and Nicholas. For a moment, only the rustling of leaves from the trees could be heard. Nicholas turned to fully face Edward, and waited. Not at all phased by Nicholas's cold hard gaze, Edward continued. "When I said it wasn't done by one of our own, I meant it was not done by one with control." Edward paused to let his words sink in. "All three girls were killed in desperation to feed. *Three* in less than a month. *All* killed by something that had not fed in a long time, and, has a taste for human blood. No one of our standing would do this simply out of respect for the laws."

Bianca's brow arched as she looked up at the taller man beside her. Her cold eyes studied him. "You think a Rogue did this?"

"I do."

"I agree with Edward." Everyone turned to look at Dominic; his black boots crushing the stones as he approached. His black leather jacket swung casually over his shoulder. "The attacks are getting more intense. First, it was taking blood and dumping the bodies. Now, it's breaking bones. It's testing itself and building up its strength. If it carries on, our very existence may be threatened." Dominic looked directly at Nicholas. "It's getting so strong and confident that it's not bothered about being found anymore."

"All Rogues were wiped out." Bianca piped up, her brow creasing.

Dominic looked at Nicholas who just stared back at him with the same knowing expression. "Not all of them," he stated. "I think it's time you contacted your family and tell them what's being happening here. *Before* this gets too out of hand."

"They're already aware. They're having a meeting as we speak," Nicholas responded, glancing slightly at Rose as she joined the group. The shaking of her head also told Nicholas that she didn't find anything either. Could it be possible? It had to be. It was the only explanation. Nicholas turned his back to everyone. "All of you go back to the college."

"What about you?" Rose asked, both curious and concerned.

"There's something I need to do. Apologise on my behalf."

Both Bianca and Edward were the first ones to nod at the instruction; Bianca linked her arm through Edward's. The pair turned and walked in unison along the path to the exit of the river. Rose took a moment to look at Nicholas before hesitantly turning and following suit. Dominic was also about to turn when Nicholas's voice stopped him.

"Would you give someone a message for me?"

Chapter Four

Charlotte just finished the last sentence as the tutor announced the end of class. Vicky had more or less nearly finished packing her things away just as Charlotte put her pen down. While massaging her wrist, Vicky leaned over eagerly. "Drinks tonight?"

Charlotte looked at Vicky with semi surprise. "I thought we agreed to stay in?"

Vicky pulled a puppy dogface and pouted her lip. "Drinks tonight?"

Charlotte just giggled at her as she packed away her things back into her handbag. Like the other students, neither of them could get out of the classroom quickly enough. The corridors were flooding quickly, everyone eager to get home and start on their Friday night sessions. While muttering to each other, Charlotte and Vicky pushed passed the crowds of students who stood near the entrance of the building. Most of them were just loitering behind hoping to gain popularity as they stood with the four most popular people in the college. Wait a minute, four? Where's Nicholas? Charlotte frowned, then just shrugged it off, not sparing another thought. It wasn't any of her business anyway. As she turned to resume her conversation with Vicky, Dominic McKnight stopped them both in their tracks. Naturally, this gave them both a bit of a shock.

"Charlotte," he said simply, eyes fixating on her.

Both Charlotte and Vicky stared for a moment at the tall, dark-haired boy before them. Then, they both slowly turned to look behind them, just to make sure Dominic was definitely talking to them. Realising that the god-like boy was most *definitely* talking to them, Charlotte quickly tucked a stray strand of hair behind her ear and nervously responded, "Yeah?"

"I'm just passing on a message from Nicholas," Dominic responded bluntly. "He wants to know if you're free tonight."

Both, Vicky and Charlotte's jaw dropped, and Charlotte's mouth went dry. For what seemed forever, the world went silent and everything began moving in slow motion. It seemed that only Charlotte, Vicky and Dominic existed in the world. The other girls from Charlotte's class stared in disbelief, already their faces turning a sour apple green with envy as they eavesdropped on the conversation.

"Nicholas wants to…" Charlotte breathed is disbelief.

"Of course she's free!" Vicky squeaked with excitement, after getting over the shock. Ignoring Charlotte's glance, she continued. "Tell Nicholas she'll meet him about eight."

Dominic looked at Vicky with slightly raised eyebrows, her tone a little too high for his sensitive hearing. He looked back at Charlotte who was still standing with her mouth wide open. "Is that alright with you?"

"Yeah." Charlotte breathed after a whole minute. Snapping out of it, she quickly cleared her throat. "Yes! Yes, that's fine. Thank you." Without another word, Dominic swung his jacket over his shoulder, turned and walked towards the other three of the group, who were waiting across the road. Charlotte waited for him to get out of earshot before turning to Vicky, who was grinning like the cat who got the cream. "*What* just happened?"

"I believe you just got a date with Mr Tall Dark and Handsome." Vicky replied, still staring in Dominic's direction. Then she patted Charlotte on the back. "Ha! Your uncle is going to love this."

Charlotte gulped the lump in her throat, trying to ignore the jealous stares, and hissing whispers around her. From the corner of her eye, she could see Stephanie Ross's disgusted glare, making the knot in her stomach even tighter. *Today is a different day after all,* she thought.

As soon as they entered the house, Bianca and Edward set up their usual game of chess in the small stone garden. The day was coming to an end. Sitting in the old metal chairs, the final ray of daylight bounced off Bianca's head, making every strand glow like a golden treasure. Edward smirked as he heard the low growl emerge from her as he took out her pawn; he glanced up and allowed his smirk to broaden.

Bianca's tiny pink lips were pursed with thought, and her perfectly shaped eyebrows were knitted together in a frown. Finally, she lifted a tiny ivory hand, and poised herself over her knight, before sliding it across the board.

"Interesting," Edward stated, staring at the knight that she had moved.

"What is?" Bianca asked, not looking up.

"Nicholas asking that girl to meet him."

Bianca just moved another pawn then looked at Edward. "Your move." Edward didn't hesitate to take another one of Bianca's pawns. With that, she leaned back in her chair in defeat and looked up into the darkening sky. "Why would he be interested in a human?" she muttered curiously.

Edward just shrugged. "Who knows? It's not the first time our kind has fallen for a human."

"Maybe his taste is beyond our kind. He is his father's son," Bianca responded with slight amusement. Bianca's expression quickly seemed to harden as she looked back at her boyfriend. Her blue jewelled eyes hard. "Do you think a Rogue has come back?"

"If it has," Edward replied, "we'll be more prepared."

Bianca just nodded slowly. "And the girl?"

Edward's seaweed green eyes also narrowed slightly. "Nicholas doesn't want her for blood or sex. He can get that anywhere. But there is something about that girl." Edward looked up to meet Bianca's gaze. "Something he is not telling us."

"You'd think after all this time, he'd trust us."

"He's a royal. He'll never trust anyone."

Bianca nodded in agreement. Nicholas was the last descendant of a rare breed. Every daughter, niece, sister or cousin was always pushed into his line of sight in the hope of securing him. The genes inherited from his father were very much sought after by the most ambitious families. But no matter how beautiful or influential, Nicholas was never seen with another female. At least not in public anyway. And yet, he was prepared to be seen with a simple human of no importance. This was interesting.

The night was starting to settle in. Edward stood from the chair and stretched out his muscles; his hunting instinct was starting to flare. He could sense Bianca was parched too. Already their eyes had adjusted to the darkening sky; like cats, their eyes were glowing with that glassy green tint. Holding out his hand, Edward helped Bianca out of the chair. For them, it was time to feed.

Chapter Five

Charlotte took a shaky sip of wine, as her eyes darted about the bar area, which was so busy and dimly lit with warm lights and flickering candles. Couples and groups of all ages were piling in, all dressed in their Friday night best. The music in the background was quiet but upbeat. People were both sitting and standing, just enjoying simple conversation. With still no sign of Nicholas, Charlotte took her little compact mirror out of her clutch bag and inspected Vicky's handy work. To be honest, Vicky didn't do a bad job. After an hour or so, both girls eventually agreed on a one-shouldered black dress with heels. Simple but classy. Charlotte ran a polished fingernail over her top and bottom lip line, making sure the red lipstick hadn't smudged. The lipstick was Vicky's, of course. Red wasn't a colour Charlotte wore often, but it definitely was the finishing touch.

"Charlotte."

Charlotte's hand froze at the familiar voice, turning her attention from her mirror, to look at the tall, finely dressed Nicholas. He literally made Charlotte take a sharp intake of breath with shock. All these years, Charlotte had *never* seen Nicholas look like this. Black trousers, white shirt with the two top buttons undone to reveal a little chest; in his hands, just a casual black jacket. The dim lights of the bar shone lines of white on his jet-black hair; the flickering candles danced in his eyes. God, he looked *gorgeous*. Charlotte could see that Nicholas had sparked flares of interest in the other women. In the background, all their greedy eyes were looking him up and down hungrily and flirtatiously. Quickly snapping out of her trance, Charlotte put her mirror away and tucked a strand of curly brown hair behind her ear. Her plump red lips curled into an awkward smile as she nervously turned to face Nicholas.

The same thoughts entered Nicholas's mind; he had never seen *her* looking so *delicious*. Nicholas took a moment to take in every detail of Charlotte, from top to bottom. Her hair had been twisted into thick plump curls, emphasising her small heart-shaped face. Like a glove, the one-shouldered black dress fitted her hourglass figure, pear drop diamond earrings dripped from her ears. And the red lipstick, which Nicholas found he was drawn to, was the finishing touch. *She looks like a queen,* Nicholas thought to himself.

Charlotte began to fidget with her dress nervously. Sensing she was feeling uncomfortable, Nicholas held out his hand. Charlotte just stared at it for moment, before gently accepting it. With no surprise, the gesture caused a few dirty looks from the women around them. As soon as their hands touched, Charlotte suddenly got that sinking feeling of danger and the need to run. But she couldn't. She daren't. Frowning, Charlotte suddenly realised that Nicholas's hand was cold. Nicholas led her to a round black table that just had one single candle that flickered excitedly as they sat. Nicholas ordered a bottle of Prosecco for the table then looked directly at Charlotte. He watched with amusement as she fiddled with her dress and stared awkwardly at her polished, crossed legs under the table. He could almost see her heart pounding through her breast. With a crooked smile, he spoke reassuringly, "You look lovely."

Charlotte looked up in surprise. After a moment, she smiled back with appreciation. "Thank you," she replied gently. "You can thank Vicky. She has good taste."

"So do you," Nicholas replied. "You looked lovely today at college. Or was that also Vicky's handy work?"

"No, that was me," Charlotte replied while letting out a little laugh. She was almost surprised that he had noticed. The waiter arrived with the Prosecco in a silver ice bucket with two glasses. Nicholas took the liberty of taking the ice bucket from the waiter and popping it in the middle of the table. Taking the bottle, he poured Charlotte a glass, but not himself. Instead, he pushed his glass to the side. "You're not drinking?" Charlotte asked with surprise as Nicholas handed her the champagne flute.

"Prosecco isn't really my thing." He replied, putting the bottle back into the silver ice bucket.

"Well, why don't you order something else?"

"I don't really drink, to be honest."

Looking around the bar, Charlotte looked back at Nicholas with a 'really?' look. "Why did you ask me to meet you in a bar then?"

Nicholas shrugged. "It's a Friday night. Why not?"

Charlotte's lips thinned, remembering something. "Where were you after lunch today? You didn't come back to class."

"I wasn't well."

"But you're well enough now? To meet up in bar?"

"I thought that's what most students did. Skive class and go out drinking."

"But you don't drink?"

Nicholas's lips curled more into a smirk as Charlotte took a quick sip of Prosecco. She was good. For a small thing, he sensed a quick-witted feisty side. Almost as quick as Bianca DeLuca, just not as deadly. Nicholas just sat and watched Charlotte from across the table, watching in fascination as she sipped at the sparkling liquid, the candle light making every bit of her glow like a beacon. She was a beauty. Nicholas's eyes fixed on her bare neck; at that point his smirk fell. "Are you happy, Charlotte?"

Charlotte paused halfway through her gulp of Prosecco, she looked at Nicholas a little confused and also surprised at his question. "What do mean? You mean here, as in the bar or—"

"I *mean*, are you happy in the college? The town? Away from your family."

"Well," Charlotte started, a little hesitant while putting the glass down. "I love English Literature, so yeah, I like the college. I love the city centre. But" – she paused, making Nicholas's eyes narrow slightly – "I think I plan to move back in with my uncle when this year is over." Nicholas quickly recalled Charlotte's uncle Carl. A dishevelled man who had been left to care for Charlotte after she lost her parents. "What about you?" Charlotte continued. "Are *you* happy?"

Nicholas remained silent for a moment, his lips thinned into a thin line before speaking. "I do miss my home," he said quietly. "I miss my mother especially. I talk to her as much as possible."

"What about your dad?"

"We don't really talk that much, to be honest."

Charlotte sensed a little sadness in his voice. "Do you not get on with him?"

"He deals with the business side of things. Always busy. So we never get a chance to talk. But, I don't really make much of an effort. We never really see eye to eye. If I do want him to know anything, I just tell my mother, who tells him."

"What is the family business? You've never said."

"That's complicated," Nicholas replied with a little hesitation. "A story for another day I'm afraid."

Charlotte nodded slowly in acceptance, but then also recalled that Nicholas was the younger of two brothers. "What about your brother?" she asked curiously. "James, is it?"

Danger. A darkness descended over the table and Nicholas's expression hardened. His jaw clenched, through his white shirt, his muscles seemed to tense. The only movement was the flickering candle in his endless black eyes.

"Dead."

Chapter Six

The atmosphere was so thick it could be cut with a knife. The music and voices, normally so energetic and upbeat, just seemed to blur into the background.

"Oh," Charlotte eventually breathed, not really knowing what to say. "Sorry."

After a moment of looking like a living statue, with only an annoyed emotion in his eyes, Nicholas just shrugged it off. "Don't worry about it. It was a long time ago."

"But, your poor mum and dad…how did they get over it? I mean, they—"

"They were heartbroken, yes. How did they get over it? Because they had to. They still had a family and a business to look after. Life goes on. After my brother" – Nicholas paused before almost whispering – "apparently I look like him."

Charlotte bit her lip awkwardly, she fidgeted in her seat. "I'm sorry," she said quietly. "If you don't mind me asking, how did he—"

"I do mind," Nicholas snapped, looking her straight in the eye. His stare were so hard and cold. "I didn't ask you to meet me just to talk about my brother."

Charlotte felt slightly shocked at Nicholas's tone; this was the Nicholas she remembered. Charlotte opened her mouth to snap back, but thought it best not to say anything. Nicholas's brother was obviously a touchy subject. Charlotte just folded her arms stubbornly and quietly asked, "Why am I here, Nicholas?"

"Because I want you to be," was the quick response, but Nicholas immediately felt that Charlotte was less than satisfied with that answer. Leaning back with almost an exhausted sigh, he tapped the table with his fingertips. "I just wanted to spend tonight with you."

"Why?"

"Because I like you."

"Like me?" Charlotte scoffed. "You've never had *anything* to do with me. You don't *know* me. And after the way you've just snapped at me, you're the last guy I even want to be around at the moment." Her pretty face twisted into more of a scowl. "You can be an arsehole sometimes."

Nicholas raised his eyebrows in surprise; that wasn't the response he'd expected at all. In all his life, he'd never really had anyone talk to him like that. Nor had he ever had a girl be hesitant or question him. But she was right. Remembering his high school years, as a boy, Nicholas kept to his own kind. In the beginning, Nicholas kept his distance. But as they got older, he began to open up a little more. Especially with Charlotte; she was so different. She had no idea how different. But Nicholas knew the risks, for her especially. Therefore, to keep her away from that life, he treated her coldly. At least, until Charlotte was ready.

Charlotte still sat straight in her chair, arms and legs crossed, still scowling. "What do you want, Nicholas?"

Nicholas looked around the bar, it had filled slightly more since they had sat down. "I wanted to ask you something," he stated, looking back her. "As you know, my family holds a big party every year. We invite family, friends, colleagues, that sort of thing. It's like a celebration of the family business." Nicholas paused, observing Charlotte's reaction. "The party is next Saturday. I'd like you to come with me."

At first, Charlotte thought he was joking. She sat silently, watching him and waiting for him to tell her the truth. But Nicholas didn't even blink. Realising that this was not a joke, Charlotte's scowl dropped to one of complete surprise. Her mahogany eyes widened in size and her mouth fell agape. "What?"

"I want you to come with me to my—"

"I heard what you said!" Charlotte interrupted in a high-pitched voice. Charlotte didn't know what to say, she just raised a hand to her pounding chest. "You asked me to meet you, so you could ask me to go to a party with you?"

"Yes."

"But," she started – her mouth was so dry – "I've never met your family! Gonna be a bit awkward, isn't it? Me walking in and—"

"You'll know me, Rose, Bianca, Dominic and Edward."

"I don't speak to *any* of them."

"Trust me," Nicholas said, leaning forward. "By the end of the night, they're the only ones you *will* want to speak to."

Charlotte couldn't believe what she was hearing. Is this really happening? Nicholas Rinaldi, is asking *her*, Charlotte Davenport, to accompany him to what had been said to be one of the classiest parties ever heard of. She'd be the envy of so many, not that she cared. God, her heart was pounding so hard, it was nearly bursting through her bones. Nicholas's brow furrowed, suddenly sensing her distress. In a flash, he was at Charlotte's feet and down on one knee. Holding her heart shaped face in between his large cool hands, their eyes locked. Brown met black. Upon contact, Charlotte felt her heart slow to a calmer beat, yet she still couldn't move. She was frozen in a trance, swimming in the deep dark depths that were Nicholas's eyes. The blood ran straight to her cheeks. Feeling her tremble at his touch, Nicholas caressed her cheeks with his thumb in a soothing circular motion. He had her right where he wanted her. His dilated eyes fell on her red lips. "Charlotte. *Please*."

"I don't have anything to wear." She whispered shakily, inches away from his face. Reaching up, Charlotte placed her small warm hands on top of Nicholas's cool ones. There it was. That was it. Every single muscle in Nicholas's body was poised for the attack. Charlotte was too close, she needed to back away. But Nicholas had a firm grip of her face. Nicholas pulled his eyes away from her lips, down to her exposed neck. *Now*. Nicholas moved one hand from Charlotte's cheek, reached around, took a thick clump of curls, and forced her face towards his. As soon as their lips touched, it set off a hot spark of electricity that flowed through them both. Charlotte's eyes at first were wide with both surprise and panic; she began to shake even more. *This is dangerous.* Charlotte's first instinct was to fight back, but then, the longer she sat in Nicholas's firm grip, the more the world just seemed to slowly disappear. Eventually, everything went black.

Chapter Seven

The room was dark. Only the silvery light from the moon came in through the wide-open curtains. With only a double bed, two side tables at each side, an oak chest of drawers, a double wardrobe, the room was plain. The silver photo frames glinting in the light were the only pretty things. Rose sat quietly on the bed in her silk cream nightgown; her thick wavy hair was freshly brushed, and her cheeks were wet with tears. This room had brought so much comfort to Rose in the past, but tonight, it was empty and lonely and cold.

Even as the bedroom door opened to reveal Dominic, she just stared blankly at him with no emotion whatsoever. Dominic paused in the doorway, meeting Rose's gaze with no surprise that she was there. With a sigh, he stepped into the room, closing the door behind him. He faced Rose, folding his arms in the process. Like a wolf in the wilderness, his eyes glowed green in the dark. Dominic stood in the light of the moon that flowed in through window, making his shirtless chest glow silver. Dominic's eyes narrowed at the sight of droplets in Rose's eyes; they glittered like diamonds. "Do you always come into his room when he's not here?"

Ignoring the question, Rose stood from the bed. "Is it true?"

"What is?"

"That girl," Rose said gulping back the lump building in her throat. "Did Nicholas meet that girl?"

Taking a few steps forward, Dominic reached up and gently wiped the fresh tears from her face. "Yes."

Rose's heart sunk into her stomach. Her pair of glowing eyes stared, heartbroken, into Dominic's. *How could he?* Rose had always been there for her lord, yet he never displayed any affection towards her in *any* public place. At first, she had been pushed by her family to get his attention. They had pushed Rose so much that she felt as though she was being suffocated by her own family. But now, Rose had built up a warm bond with Nicholas since they had started college together. Leaning forward, Rose put her head onto Dominic's chest. "Why?" she wept.

"Because, he…" Dominic started but found that he couldn't finish the sentence. Because the truth was, he didn't understand it himself. "Rose," Dominic started again, putting his cold hands on her slender shoulders. "You've always been loyal. You've always been there whenever he needed you." He paused for a moment. "You're a good girl to both Nicholas and your family. But you deserve so much better than *this*. The feelings you want from him…" he trailed off as Rose stiffened underneath his hands. His lips thinned into a line. "He can't give them to you. And for that, on Nicholas's behalf, I am sorry."

Rose stood deadly still, then after the words sank in, she pulled away from Dominic. The tears had stopped, she had no more to give. There was no movement from her, like a living statue. The glow in her eyes suddenly became gold and dangerous. After a moment, she managed to utter the words in a low, husky voice. "But he will give them to a human girl."

Dominic looked sympathetic at her, opened his mouth to try and utter words of comfort but was stopped by a familiar sound. Quickly turning his head to glance behind him, he saw Nicholas standing in the doorway of the room. Like a wolf, Nicholas's lips had pulled back to reveal his crystal white teeth in a semi snarl. A low growl escaped from his throat as a warning. Normally, the young Prince was so calm and collected, but this had triggered his defence. How dare Rose! All those nights he had spent with her, allowing her to enter his room without permission, allowing her to lay in his bed. No other female got close like Rose did. In the midst of all these privileges, she seemed to have forgotten that Nicholas Rinaldi was still a royal. Therefore, still *her* superior.

"I apologise, my Lord," Rose spoke quietly, acknowledging the growl. Rose didn't even look at Nicholas. "I spoke out of turn. It won't happen again."

"You're right," Nicholas growled dangerously. "It won't."

Without another word, Rose simply walked silently past Dominic and Nicholas, her silk cream nightgown trailing behind her. Even when Rose opened and closed it with a slight bang, Nicholas paid no attention.

"Does she know?" Dominic asked.

"No." Nicholas responded simply.

Then, both Nicholas and Dominic exchanged the same look. Their sensitive sense of smell had been attracted to something else. There was a scent of fresh blood in the air.

Vicky jumped up from the sofa, nearly spilling her camomile tea, as she heard the front door open. Dressed in her pyjamas and her hair in a messy bun, Vicky dashed straight into the hallway. Seeing her masterpiece step into the house, Vicky's eyes doubled with excitement. "Well?" she asked eagerly.

Charlotte smiled at her friend with amusement as she closed the door behind her and kicked off her heels. "It was…interesting."

"Interesting…?" Vicky repeated slowly with an arched eyebrow. "*Just* interesting?"

Charlotte nodded as she headed into the cream painted living room. She plopped down into the large armchair and began massaging her feet. Vicky followed close behind and laid back on the sofa, putting her camomile tea on the coffee table. "So." She continued looking at Charlotte curiously. "What happened then?"

"Nothing much to be honest," Charlotte replied, taking out her earrings. "We talked, we—*I* drank, we kissed, he invited me to his family party, then we decided to head—"

"Whoa, whoa," Vicky interrupted quickly, sitting up straight and pointing her palm in Charlotte's direction, signalling for her to halt. "You've been invited to *the* Rinaldi Ball?"

"The what?"

"Rinaldi Ball? It's like the biggest event *ever*! Trust me, our prom will be nothing compared to this party. You know the red carpet event?" Vicky asked; when Charlotte nodded, she continued. "Well, it's like that, but bigger, classier, richer and *definitely* more glamourous. There's big money at that party. Hey, you could meet a nice, rich husband!"

Charlotte stared at Vicky with a little surprise. She had heard that the Rinaldi's put on a good party, but she never once thought that it was this big. *I suppose I should feel honoured,* Charlotte thought to herself. Touching her lips, Charlotte remembered the kiss. The feeling of Nicholas's touch as he pleaded with her to be his partner at the party. But that kiss was definitely something out of this world. Nicholas even suggested introducing her to his parents which was a shock. Out of the all the others he could have chosen, he chose *her*. Charlotte began chewing her lip in thought; she felt so strange. The sickening and panicky feeling came over Charlotte, as though she was lost in a dream. But she wasn't lost, she sat with Vicky, in their cream painted living room, in their shared house.

"Mate," Vicky continued excitedly. "You are *so* lucky. So many girls would give anything to be you right now."

"Yeah, great." Charlotte shrugged, trying to shift the sick feeling in her stomach. "Problem is, I'm just not one of them."

"But, he asked you—"

"He asked me to go the party, nothing else."

"But he kissed you, right?" Vicky replied. When Charlotte nodded, she smirked. "Want me to send the roses back?"

"Roses?" Charlotte repeated with a frown, looking at her friend.

Still smirking, Vicky picked up her camomile tea and nodded in the hallway's direction. "Kitchen table."

Curious, Charlotte quickly stood from the armchair, rushed through the short length of the hallway and into, the almost tidy kitchen. *Whoa*. There, on the oak kitchen table, was the biggest bunch of the most beautiful ruby red roses that Charlotte had ever seen.

Chapter Eight

Saturday afternoon was brighter than the day before, and Charlotte had woken up with a more lively feeling and a bounce in her step. While driving into the city and even taking a seat at the restaurant table, Uncle Carl had asked a number of times what caused Charlotte to be so chirpy. Charlotte just casually brushed off her uncle's curiosity and just put it down to the first cup of coffee she'd had that morning. Taking her mirror, she checked her hair that had been neatly brushed back into a ponytail.

Compared to Charlotte, Carl Davenport's colouring was completely different. His sandy blonde hair was dishevelled and greying, and he always liked to keep a bit of stubble on his face. While Charlotte had warm, round brown eyes, Carl's eyes were cool, round and blue. Carl was a funny and loving man and after Charlotte, football and beer were his second love. At least when he wasn't working anyway. Although, to this day, Charlotte still wasn't sure what her uncle did for a living. All she knew was that he dealt with security for big companies. But to be honest, Charlotte didn't care about the details; Carl had worked so hard to provide for her while she was growing up. Charlotte was the apple of his eye.

"What's this?" she asked as her uncle slid a white envelope across the table. Quickly, she put her mirror back into her handbag.

Carl just grinned his usual goofy grin. "Open it and find out."

Looking curiously at her uncle, she carefully ripped it open. Trying not to damage whatever was inside. As soon as Charlotte saw the thick wad of cash, she quickly slammed the envelope back on the table and looked at her uncle sternly. "No!"

"Take it!"

"Uncle Carl, *no*."

"Please."

"No!"

"You can use it to find somewhere else to live for the time being."

"I'm not looking to find anywhere else to live, though."

"Well, now you can start looking can't you?" Carl's grin seemed to drop slightly as he became more serious. "Just take it." He paused for moment, but he could see Charlotte struggling to make a decision. "*Please.*"

"I thought you liked where I lived?" Charlotte questioned with a frown and a pout.

"I did. But that was before girls started going missing around your area. Please take it, it'll give me some peace of mind."

Charlotte hesitated, tutting and rolling her eyes, she picked up the envelope and stuffed into her handbag. "Thanks."

Carl nodded with approval at her while waiter cleared away the plates. Once again, Charlotte pulled out her compact mirror to check her hair and makeup. Carl watched curiously with both a smirk and arched eyebrow. Charlotte had been doing this since she left the house; something was different. Today she was glowing. Every time Carl had asked what was going on, she had just shrugged. But he couldn't take it anymore. He wanted an answer. "Alright, that's it!" he announced, earning a surprised look from his niece. Quickly putting her mirror away, Charlotte giggled as her uncle leaned in across the table to look her in the eye. "What's his name?"

Charlotte just shrugged innocently. "It's no big deal, Uncle Carl."

"That's an unusual name!"

Charlotte just laughed even more. "Seriously," she said through giggles. "It's nothing big."

Her uncle's smirk broadened into a cheesier grin. "Well, 'nothing big', doesn't make you check your face three times an hour." Carl paused a minute to stare at his niece before speaking again excitedly. "Come on! Who is he?"

Charlotte just simply smiled. "Nicholas."

"Nicholas…?"

"Rinaldi."

Carl's cheesy grin fell immediately from his face. Time, like Charlotte's uncle, suddenly seemed to freeze like ice. Usually the warm and gentle Carl, suddenly became stern and serious. "When did you see him last?" he asked.

Confused, Charlotte leaned back and tilted her head in concern. There were very few occasions where Charlotte felt nervous about being around her uncle. But his whole body became rigid and frosty. "L-last night," Charlotte replied, also feeling a hard lump in her throat. "W-why? Is—"

Carl's sky blue eyes narrowed. "Did he touch you?" he snapped.

Charlotte vigorously shook her head. "No! Well, he did but it—" Charlotte was stopped midsentence by Carl suddenly sitting upright in his chair, his face a mixed expression of shock, fury and horror. Quickly, Charlotte reached over and touched his hand, squeezing it reassuringly. "No! Nothing like *that* happened. It was…just a kiss."

Carl was frozen in his seat; Charlotte was very confused and worried at this point. She could tell he was grinding his teeth by the circular motion of his cheekbones. Carl had always been protective when it came to boys, but he'd never reacted like this. This looked like pure white fear. After a moment, Carl spoke again, his voice still very low. "Just a kiss?"

Charlotte once again nodded vigorously, squeezing his hand even tighter, trying desperately to reassure him that a kiss was *all* that happened. "Just a kiss…Promise!" Carl's narrow eyes remained frozen on her face for a moment or two, then finally, he blinked, and relaxed. He leaned over the table and folded his arms. Feeling thankful, Charlotte let out the breath that she didn't even realise she'd been holding. Releasing Carl's hand, Charlotte leaned back into her chair and folded her own arms. "Do…Do you know them?"

Carl nodded slightly, his face starting to look less stern. "Well," he said calmly. "I wouldn't go that far. I don't *know* them, know them. I've heard of them and probably met them once or twice in the past."

"Did you know their son? James?"

"Yeah. I met him."

Charlotte chewed her lip for a moment, choosing her words carefully. "Nicholas said he died."

"Well, that's the story that went around," Carl replied, while stroking his stubbly face. Once again, his eyes narrowed. "What else did Nicholas say to you?"

"How?" Charlotte asked again curiously, ignoring her uncle's question.

Carl shrugged. "No one knows. James's disappearance was one of the most talked about things ever. One minute he was there, the next, he just disappeared. When he wasn't found, they had to call off the search and proclaim him dead." Carl's face dropped with sadness slightly. "Absolutely broke William and Elise's heart."

"William and Elise?"

"James and Nicholas's mother and father—" Carl stopped and awkwardly ran a hand through his sandy hair. He looked at Charlotte with a little worry in his eyes. "Charlotte, honey, I've got to be honest. I don't really like the idea of you seeing Nicholas. That family…they're not like any other."

Charlotte was a little taken back by her uncle. She knew he didn't like the idea of her going out with other boys, but he never commented. This was something new. Trying to convince herself it was just Carl's protective instinct. Charlotte once again, reassuringly, put a hand on her uncle's hand. "I'll be fine," she said smiling softly. "It's nearly the end of the year. I probably won't see him again after college."

Even as Carl smiled back and placed his hand on top of Charlotte's, he couldn't help but feel a little less optimistic.

Chapter Nine

Children could be heard playing giddily in the park area, their parents watching in awe from the benches as they talked amongst themselves. Dog walkers, runners, couples of all ages were making the most of the clear sky. For August, the weather was surprisingly warm and light.

In the woodland area, not far from the playground, Rose walked casually along the dry muddied path. The children's high-pitched squeals, pounding feet from the runners and panting of the dogs, created a collage of sounds in Rose's ears.

Walking down the stone steps and under the stone archway, Rose continued to walk deeper into the trees, the sounds began to fade. Only the breeze, and the crunching of stones and leaves beneath her boots could be heard. Apart from, of course, the odd whistle and crow from the birds above. Stopping in the clearing, Rose quickly glanced around to check her surroundings, her pinpoint pupils scanning *everything*. Looking up and down the grey stone steps, up the tiny steep hill where the trees, nearly bare, leaned over sadly. Taking a few steps forward, Rose also looked down and checked the other set of stone steps, which led down to the edge of the park and to the river. The wide, swirling strip of water could be seen down below.

Satisfied that the coast was clear, Rose looked up, and like a panther, pounced up into the air to an incredible height. The first tree she could grip, Rose dug her sharp nails into its dry hard bark and held on with little effort. Beneath her boots, the branches rustled and shook; the breeze became more aggressive at the top. Rose held on with one hand and brought the other to her lips, and bit down. The skin burned as her canines punctured her skin, copper tasting fluid was now flowing into Rose's mouth. Convinced she had enough, Rose reached out, palm facing down, and let the ruby liquid drip on to the branches and the ground below. Facing the bark, she also spat the blood in her mouth onto the tree. After a couple of minutes, Rose pulled her hand back in as her hand began to heal. Now, we wait.

Getting properly balanced, Rose knelt down onto the branch and stared down at the ground below her. Wiping her mouth and licking her lips. The scent of Rose's fresh blood blew into the breeze.

Surprisingly, it wasn't long before Rose's eye caught movement between the branches. An elderly man was walking towards the tree, walking stick in hand. He looked absolutely tiny and so frail. Yet he still managed to get down the hill? Rose watched with beady narrow eyes. The elderly man stopped dead at the base of the tree and just stared down for a minute or two. Then, throwing his stick down into the rotten leaves, he dived head first into the base trunk. Aggressively, he ripped the bark from the tree, the sounds he was making were distorted and snarling.

Rose released the tree and, like a cat, landed perfectly on both feet, her boots crushing the crisp dead leaves beneath her.

Hearing her, the old man's head snapped up in surprise to look behind him. Rose's face twisted in disgust at the disgusting sight before her. Hunched over like a monkey, the old man's face was covered in bark, blood, dried dirt and leaves. His teeth protruding over his bottom lip; his face twisted with both wrinkles and madness. Acknowledging Rose for a moment, his lips soon curled up like the joker and he laughed huskily.

"Something funny?" Rose hissed.

The old man began to sing a sickly sweet song. "Naughty, naughty. Clever, clever. You tricked me. You caught me. You—" His song soon stopped and his face suddenly fell.

Nicholas, Dominic, Bianca and Edward landed from the treetops and joined Rose at her side. The old man was now staring in shock, horror and fear. The realisation he had been caught, hit. The old man's eyes were wide, grey and blood shot. Despite his obvious fear, he twisted his body around and continued to sit like a monkey. His eyes flicked from Bianca, to Edward, to Dominic, to Rose then finally, just to freeze on Nicholas. The old man stopped shaking; he just stared blankly at Nicholas. Then out of nowhere, he just simply looked up into the trees and howled. "Nicholas Rinaldi!"

Nicholas didn't even flinch. "So, you do know who I am."

The old man stopped howling. All the fear drained from his face. That sick, joker smile came back. "Oh I know *you*," he said huskily, looking back at Nicholas. "You're the *Prince*. The *fake* Prince."

"Fake?" Nicholas questioned arching his eyebrow. "The last time I checked, I was the second son born—"

"You are a traitor to your kind!" The old man spat, blood and saliva frothing from his mouth. "A *rare* breed with unlimited power. But you never use it. Instead, you encourage peace with *them*." The old man paused to spit blood at Nicholas's feet. "You would sacrifice your own, for *them*. You weak little boy."

Nicholas just continued to stare, emotionless. "Tell me," he said finally, "who killed those girls?"

The old man once again just smiled and tilted his head sideways. "Not me."

"Who did?"

"Not me!"

"Was it a Rogue?"

"They were *so* polite," the man said in a high pitched, sweet voice. "Helping an old man. You never get young people helping old people these days. They were *so* pretty, and *sweet*. It was so easy and beautiful to watch."

"Who killed them?" Nicholas repeated.

"They look pretty too." The old man said, glancing in the direction of the playground where the blurred squeals of the children could be heard.

Growls escaped from the lips of Nicholas, Bianca, Dominic, Rose and Edward; like a pride of lions, they became rigid and ready. Nicholas took a step forward. "For the final time," he growled, revealing his protruding teeth. "*Who killed*—?"

"Not me! Not me! Not me! Not me! Not—" The old man sang. Snarling, Nicholas darted towards the old man and went straight for the throat. He had finally lost his patience. Gripping his fragile neck, Nicholas lifted the man off the ground so he was eye level with him. Nicholas's teeth were long, white, sharp and bare. The old man's empty grey eyes were large and almost filling with tears at the sight of the prince's fury. "Don't hurt me," he managed to choke out. "I'm an old man."

"*You*," Nicholas growled. "*Who* are you working for? This is your last chance. Tell me!" Nicholas paused before snarling aggressively. "*Now!*"

The old man just began to laugh and choke within the prince's grip. Staring into Nicholas's burning gaze, he whispered. "I heard *you* like human girls too." He laughed even harder despite Nicholas's tightening grip. "That's a shame. My master likes Charlotte too."

"Enough of this." Edward growled appearing at Nicholas's side. Slamming his pointed fingers straight through the old man's chest, his hand burst straight through the other side. Edwards hand, arm, and jacket were now soaked, dripping and red. The old man didn't get a chance to howl in agony as Nicholas quickly released the man's throat. Bianca dived and ripped his head cleanly from his body. Bouncing immediately off the tree, she avoided the spray of blood that came towards her. The body slid from Edward's arm to the ground; the brown leaves soon turned black as the blood began to soak in. In her hands, Bianca held the head by the sliver of snow-white hair.

Chapter Ten

Most of the class was crowded around Bethany Croft, muttering and whispering amongst themselves. Some of the girls were rubbing her back and even giving her long, comforting hugs. The students who couldn't get close to her, were kneeling on their desks trying to listen in on the conversation, and some simply stood in small groups looking at newspapers.

"What's wrong with Beth?" Vicky asked with concern as she dropped her bag onto her desk. Vicky had noticed that Bethany's face was red and puffy.

"Don't know," Charlotte replied, also looking with concern at the small crowd at the front of the class. Charlotte quickly looked around and noticed Tom stood alone with a newspaper. "Tom!" she called, trying not to be too loud. Charlotte waited for him to look up before waving him over. Tom folded the paper and briskly walked over. Charlotte nodded in Bethany's direction. "What's going on?"

Tom's lips thinned sadly as he unfolded the paper again and showed both Vicky and Charlotte the headline. "They've found Louisa."

Both Charlotte and Vicky leaned in closer to the article, reading the heading quickly.

A fourth victim found. Louisa Croft, twenty, has been found dead near the train lines. Last seen out with friends on Saturday night when she disappeared.

"Oh no," Vicky muttered, not able to take her eyes off the picture.

"I know," Tom replied sadly. "It's the worst one. Beth said whoever did this, ripped her throat open and literally crushed her skeleton."

"Oh my God," Vicky breathed in disbelief, glancing at Charlotte. "That's…that's *awful*."

Tom nodded his head slowly in agreement; Charlotte looked at Beth whose head was in her hands, her body trembling as she cried. More members of the class wrapped their arms more tightly around her. Louisa was Bethany's older sister. The two were thick as thieves, always shopping together, always having lunch together, always studying together. While Beth was a slightly chubby, light brown haired girl, Louisa had been thin and blonde. Biting her lip, Charlotte made her way to the front of the class. Politely, pushing past the other students, Charlotte gently put a warm hand on Beth's shoulder. "Beth," she whispered softly. She waited for the teary-eyed girl look at her. "I'm…I'm really sorry, to hear about Louisa."

With tears streaming down her face and her lips trembling, Beth could do nothing but nod her head in appreciation. Her light brown eyes dropped slightly. "Thanks," she choked out. "It's been a shock, obviously." Charlotte nodded as she comfortingly rubbed her back. Beth continued. "It's her birthday next week. We had a party planned. We were going to take her to her favourite restaurant." Beth paused as tears once again built up her eyes. "I booked a room at her favourite bar. All our family was going to be there. I just…I just don't understand. Why would someone do this to Louisa? She never did anything to anyone! She was just trying to get through university. Why?" Beth was practically screaming now. "Why would someone do this? Why! *Why! Why!"* With that, Beth put her head in her hands and cried uncontrollably.

Not knowing what to do, Charlotte was grateful when the English Literature tutor walked briskly into the room. Clearly, the tutor had been informed of Beth's loss by the way she wrapped her arm around her. Gently, the tutor guided the crying girl out of class, calmly whispering words of comfort. Charlotte could do nothing more, other than sadly stare in their direction. As the classroom door closed, the room became its usual gossiping, buzzing beehive.

"Is it true you went on a date with Nicholas?"

Charlotte's head snapped back to look at Stephanie Ross. The auburn haired girl with catty green eyes and a face packed with makeup. "What?"

Stephanie stood in the middle of a small group of girls who, before now, had been quietly muttering amongst themselves. Now, all their judgemental eyes were now fixed on Charlotte. Others in the class also stopped their own conversations at Stephanie's words, who tutted with annoyance at having to repeat herself. "Did *you* go on a *date* with *Nicholas*?"

Charlotte frowned at the other girl's tone; choosing to ignore it, Charlotte replied. "Yes *I* did."

"So," Stephanie continued, looking Charlotte up and down, "you two are like, a *thing*, now?"

The class waited with baited breath as Charlotte carefully chose the right words. Trying to ignore the burning to her cheeks, Charlotte continued to stare Stephanie straight in the eye. "No."

The corners of Stephanie's lips seemed to curl upward with a tiny smirk. Looking Charlotte up and down, once again. "Didn't think so." She muttered as she turned to face the rest of her group.

"And what's that supposed to mean?" Charlotte snapped, ignoring the giggles from the other girls.

Smirking, Stephanie turned back around. "Oh, nothing," she said in a fake, innocent voice. "You just, don't seem like his type to be honest."

"And let me guess, *you* are?"

"Well." Stephanie shrugged. "I wouldn't say that. But, it's my birthday soon. I'm planning on—"

"Excuse me!" Vicky interrupted as she made her way to the front of the class. She pointed a finger straight at Stephanie. "*You* haven't got a chance." Vicky then pointed her finger at Charlotte. "Charlotte, has been invited to the *Rinaldi Ball*."

Gasps of breath could be heard from every direction of the classroom. Charlotte could feel all eyes burning into her more intensely now. Stephanie's face fell with a mixture of both shock and anger. "You're a liar!" she hissed.

Charlotte put her head in her hands, completely embarrassed and not knowing what to do, she prayed for Vicky to stop talking. She prayed for the spotlight to be taken off her. But Vicky being Vicky, just stood tall like a triumphant conqueror, and grinned like a Cheshire cat as she met Stephanie's glare. "No, I'm not."

"Nobody gets invited to that party! That's a party for important people," Stephanie snapped, then looked straight back at Charlotte. Her green eyes became sharp slits. "*She's not important! Look at her!*"

Appalled by that comment, Vicky growled and began immediately rolling up her sleeves, but was stopped dead.

"Wrong," a voice interrupted, making all heads snap. Walking in, Dominic, Rose, Bianca and Edward casually strode into class and towards their usual seats at the back. They didn't take any notice of the scene occurring before them. Nicholas however, was standing so close to Charlotte they were practically touching; his sight fixed on Stephanie. "I'm sorry, but you're wrong," his voice so serious that Charlotte detected a little anger. "Charlotte is very important. If she wasn't, I wouldn't have asked her to meet me on Friday night. She is so important, you can't even begin to imagine. And I most *certainly,* would *not* have asked her to the Rinaldi Ball." The silence in the room was deafening as everyone stared wide-eyed at Nicholas's grand statement. Even Dominic, Rose, Bianca and Edward exchanged glances. Stephanie shifted awkwardly under Nicholas's intense gaze. After at least a minute or two, Nicholas averted his gaze from Stephanie to look at Charlotte. "I'll send a driver around to pick you up on Friday evening. We'll be staying at my parents' house."

With a slightly open mouth and wide eyes, Charlotte could only utter one word. "Okay."

Without another word, Nicholas turned, the rest of the class parting like the Red Sea as he joined the rest of his group at the back of the class. Charlotte watched with a mixture of shock, embarrassment and gratitude. Stephanie just stood awkwardly in the centre of the class, biting her lip.

Chapter Eleven

The rest of the week seemed to fly by and Friday night had come. With Vicky nearly breaking the speed limit, Charlotte was home, bags packed and ready to go in no time. As Nicholas had promised, he sent a driver to pick Charlotte up. Both Charlotte and Vicky watched with excitement and curiosity as the black Audi pulled in front of the house. Although, while Vicky was definitely more excited, Charlotte was more curious. The driver politely introduced himself as Ratcliffe, then kindly took her bag. After saying her goodbyes to Vicky, and not long after setting off, Charlotte soon found herself on the twisting bumpy roads of the countryside. The tall silver, shiny buildings of the city blurring into the background, and Charlotte was alone.

Everywhere Charlotte looked, bare brown fields surrounded her; the soil had been overturned by the tractors readying them for the next harvest. As Ratcliffe continued to drive silently further into the farmland areas, the plain brown fields soon turned green. Sheep and cows grazed contentedly in their fields, and while they seemed to be at peace; Charlotte couldn't help but feel the opposite.

"Here we are." Ratcliffe simply stated. They were the only words he had said since they had set off.

The uneasy feeling soon lifted, as Charlotte quickly looked out of the backseat window and gasped. The Audi pulled up to a tall metal gate which opened as soon as they came within two metres. Once the gates opened, Ratcliffe slowly drove the car up a long driveway. Charlotte took a minute to admire her surroundings. Finely trimmed green grass hemmed the driveway, pink apple blossom trees stood tall around the edges of the garden, almost hiding the white wall surrounding the house. In the centre, a white marbled tiered fountain stood elegantly, with crystal clear water trickling down. As they got closer, Charlotte had to tilt her head further back; the red brick and limestone house looked so grand and bright amongst its green scenery. Pulling the Audi up against the steps, Charlotte noticed the wooden door of the house open and Nicholas stepped out. Once again, he was wearing a black turtleneck jumper and dark jeans, and as usual, looking so relaxed. Unbuckling her seat belt, and quickly getting out of the car, Charlotte met Nicholas half way up the stone steps.

Nicholas immediately wrapped his arms around her. "Welcome." He muttered with a smile.

Charlotte held him for a moment, before pulling away. She then gazed around the scenery around the front of the house. "Am I at the Rinaldi home, or Buckingham Palace? This is stunning!" she exclaimed with a smile.

"Thank you," Nicholas replied, looking around. "My mother took a lot of time designing it."

"Your mum" – Charlotte breathed in shock – "designed *this*?"

Laughing slightly, Nicholas took Charlotte's hand and led her into the house. Ratcliffe followed silently with her bag.

Nicholas led Charlotte into the wide-open mahogany and white foyer, with a staircase straight ahead which lead to the first floor of the house. Above their heads, a bohemian crystal chandelier glittered. On the right hand side, the door was open, and Charlotte guessed that was the dining room by the tip of mahogany table and chair. However, the door on the left was closed.

"Whoa," she breathed in awe. "This is incredible. It's like something out of a magazine."

"Like it?" Nicholas asked, smiling even more as he watched her reaction.

Charlotte nodded. "It's amazing! How many rooms?"

"Twelve, but that's not including the dining room and sitting room."

"Who cleans them all?"

"We have a few maids that live here with us."

"And drivers," Charlotte said, hinting at Ratcliffe. "I feel sorry for the cleaner though. It must take—"

"Is it an old house?"

Nicholas joined Charlotte in looking around the foyer. "It's been in my family for a very long time."

"How long?"

"At a guess, since the thirteen hundreds."

"Ah," Charlotte replied. "Renaissance period."

Nicholas looked at Charlotte with surprise. "You knew that?"

Charlotte grinned up at Nicholas. "I paid attention in history."

"Nicholas!" a female voice suddenly shouted. Both Nicholas and Charlotte looked up to a see a white-blonde haired woman walking along the first floor. While reading the magazine, she began walking down the staircase. "Nicholas, for tomorrow, I want you to be—" The woman looked up, and stopped midsentence. The woman was small with soft white-blonde hair, and her eyes were a peculiar peppermint green. She wore a bright pink blouse, grey trousers and black heels. A delicate pearl necklace hung around her pale neck. She was beautiful. She folded the magazine and smiled politely at Charlotte. "Oh, I do apologise!" she said cheerily. "I wasn't expecting anyone so early!"

Nicholas cleared his throat. "Charlotte, this is my mum, Elise Rinaldi." Nicholas hesitated for a moment. "Mum, this is Charlotte Davenport. A friend from college."

Elise's eyes widened and her eyebrows raised. She quickly opened her mouth to say something, but Nicholas's expression told her not to say anything. Not here. With a smile, Elise looked back at the brown-haired girl that stood nervously in her foyer. Politely, Elise held out her hand. "Pleased to meet you, Charlotte."

"And you," Charlotte replied quickly, accepting Elise's handshake.

"So," Elise continued, "you're a student of English Literature too? What brings you here? It's a long way from the city just to make a flying visit."

"She's not making a flying visit," Nicholas said quickly before Charlotte even opened her mouth. Elise looked at him with a frown. "I invited Charlotte to our ball tomorrow night."

A silence filled the foyer, so thick it could be cut with a knife. "*What?*" Elise hissed in disbelief, her eyes shooting daggers at her son.

Charlotte's lips thinned, she slowly looked up at Nicholas with realisation. "You didn't even ask if I could come, did you?"

Nicholas looked down at Charlotte, reaching up, he stroked her hair. "Because I knew it wouldn't be a problem."

"You still could have told me!" Elise exclaimed waving her arms around. "Where will the poor girl sleep?"

"Here."

"*Here?*" Elise put her head in her hands in despair. "Oh, God have mercy…"

"I am not sleeping here!" Charlotte snapped.

"Where will you go then?" Nicholas asked. "There's no hotels or bed and—"

"I am so sorry!" Charlotte piped up in a panicky squeaky voice, looking back at Elise. "I swear, I thought you knew! I promise, I would never have just come here without permission."

Elise reached over and took Charlotte's hand reassuringly. "*You* don't have to apologise for *anything*," she said softly. "*I* should be the one apologising to *you* for my reaction. Honestly, it would be nice to have you join us tomorrow. It'll be a nice change to have someone different there. Someone who's not involved in business anyway. I have the perfect room for you, if you'd still like to stay?" Charlotte hesitated for a moment or two, but Elise's comforting and warm gaze was just a little too much to resist. Charlotte grinned and nodded. Elise smiled happily, then sternly looked at Nicholas. "While I take Charlotte to her room, *you* can tell your father."

Nicholas nodded in obedience at his mother as she took Charlotte by the hand and led her up the staircase. Charlotte was led into a bright, white painted hallway where smaller chandeliers hung from the ceiling. Small mahogany tables with vases of roses lined the edges of both sides. Doors were on either side and Elise stopped at the door at the end. Opening it, she stepped inside and flicked on the light. Stepping to the side, Elise allowed Charlotte to enter after her. Once again, Charlotte grinned at the stunning decor.

"I hope you'll be comfortable." Elise said softly.

"This is…perfect," Charlotte said, smiling. "Thank you so much."

"Well then, I'll let you get settled." Elise began to close the door. "Let me know if you need anything."

Charlotte nodded as Elise closed the door, she began to observe her room in more detail. The room was large with a mahogany four-poster bed, two side drawers at either side. On the opposite side of the room, there was a mahogany wardrobe and dressing table with a single chair. The bedroom window faced the garden, and the window seat was padded with soft red velvet.

Charlotte opened the bathroom door to be greeted by blinding white marble. A freshly polished shower, bath, and sink. Charlotte walked back into the bedroom and took a seat at the window, and looked down at the flowing fountain. Smiling, she watched a family of rabbits scurry across the bright green grass. Everything about this place was beautiful, and yet, it was almost like a dream. Once again, a strange feeling came over Charlotte. *Why am I here?* She thought.

Chapter Twelve

The Rinaldi Ball had come, and guests had started arriving.

Charlotte sat at her dressing table, watching intently as the maid fixed her hair into a half up, half down style, with delicate curls trailing down her back. Using small diamond pins, the maid firmly pinned Charlotte's mahogany hair into place. The dress was laid neatly on the four-poster bed, something else that Nicholas had arranged.

Knocking slightly on the door, Elise popped her head in with a smile. "How are we getting on?"

Charlotte's jaw dropped as Elise almost glided into her room. She was wearing a silk, emerald green dress, her white blonde hair had been put into a low bun with a crystal leaf and wreath comb. Around her neck, a wreath diamond necklace to match. Elise looked like royalty. "You look stunning!"

"Oh, thank you, dear," Elise replied, straightening out her dress. "Well, I just came to tell you that all our guests are nearly here, so please, come down when you're ready."

"Where's Nicholas?" Charlotte asked curiously. "I haven't seen him for a while."

"He's getting ready with William. Don't worry, he won't be long."

Elise then turned and headed back out of the room, leaving the maid to help Charlotte into the dress. Surprisingly, Nicholas had very good taste, for he had chosen a satin, magenta purple, fishtail dress, with off the shoulder sleeves. Complimented by a pair of simple diamond earrings. *Well, this is as good as it's going to get,* Charlotte thought, looking herself up and down in the mirror. Thanking the maid, Charlotte headed for the door, holding the dress up off the floor slightly. Stepping out of her room, Charlotte suddenly stopped at seeing the familiar figure, also making his way out of a room a bit further up from Charlotte's. "Uncle Carl?"

Carl turned in surprise at his name; he stared wide-eyed at Charlotte, as though he had seen a ghost. Charlotte looked him up and down with a frown. What was he wearing? Black boots, black trousers, a long black trench coat and over his black jumper, a stab proof vest. He looked like a vigilante. Before Charlotte knew it, Carl was in front of her, gripping her shoulders a little too hard. Glaring in horror down at her. "What the hell are you doing *here*?" he asked angrily.

"I got invited by Nicholas," Charlotte replied, confused. "What are *you* doing here?"

"I'm doing the security for William."

"You do security for the Rinaldis?"

"Charlotte, I *told* you to stay away!"

"No, you didn't. You said you weren't happy—"

"Don't give me that," Carl growled. He let go of Charlotte and ran his hand, exasperated, through his sandy hair. Then, he looked up the hallway, then with sudden panic took a firm hold of her wrist and began to lead Charlotte back into the bedroom. "Pack your things, you're going home."

"What? No!"

"Don't argue with me, Charlotte. Just do it."

Charlotte tried to pull out of her uncle's grip. "What's your problem?"

"You don't want to be here, trust me."

"Yes, I do! I'm only staying for the weekend then I'll be back home." Charlotte dug her heels as hard as she could. "Uncle Carl, let go of me!"

"You're not staying the weekend, you're going home *now*."

"Mr Davenport."

Charlotte and Carl stopped dead to see Nicholas standing behind them, wearing his black and white dinner suit. One hand, casually hanging out of his jacket pocket. Carl took a step in front of Charlotte and pushed her behind him protectively. "Nicholas," he growled. "You should have told me that you'd invited Charlotte."

"I didn't realise I needed to ask permission to invite *my* friends to *my* house."

"Wait," Charlotte said, pushing past her uncle. "You two know each other?"

Carl didn't break eye contact with Nicholas. "I do security for them on the odd occasion. Large parties mainly."

"You said you only met them once or twice?" Charlotte questioned, frowning.

Carl looked down at her sternly "That's true. Whenever they have an important party, my company is always asked to be there to make sure things run smoothly."

"And a very good job you do too," Nicholas stated, making Carl look back at him coldly. From Nicholas's tone, Charlotte got the impression that Nicholas was mocking her uncle. The classical music could be heard playing in the background downstairs, but even that didn't soothe the thickening atmosphere. Nicholas looked at Charlotte, taking a moment to congratulate himself on the dress that he had picked for her, before holding out his hand. "Shall we?"

As Charlotte reached to accept it, Carl grabbed Nicholas's hand. "Nicholas," he growled.

"Oh, I'm sorry," Nicholas said, smiling mockingly. "Do I have your permission?"

"Yes, you do!" Charlotte piped up, glaring at her uncle who looked down at her with pleading blue eyes. Ignoring him, Charlotte took Nicholas's hand and together they walked, or in Charlotte's case, marched, down the hallway and down the stairs. The brightly lit foyer, now a dance floor, was packed with the most glamorously dressed people Charlotte had ever seen. Tables and chairs had been set up around the room with white tablecloths and silver candelabra centre pieces. A small orchestra had been set up near the back, and their music played exquisitely in the background. Charlotte noticed other men and women dressed in the same uniform as her uncle, but they stood like living statues in every corner of the room. "I'm sorry about my uncle," Charlotte continued as Nicholas led her into a dance. "I'm not sure what that was about."

"Protective uncle," Nicholas said politely. "It's understandable. I would have probably reacted the same if it was my niece or daughter."

"So, you want kids one day?"

"One day," Nicolas replied as he twirled Charlotte. "But not yet."

"Waiting for the right girl to come along?"

"If she hasn't already."

Charlotte licked her lips and looked at Nicholas curiously. "In class, you said I was important. What did you mean by that?"

Nicholas didn't respond, instead he landed a butterfly kiss on her forehead, making her completely oblivious to the whispers and stares around her. Next to them, Bianca and Edward were dancing like professionals. Bianca's royal blue teacup dress emphasised her tiny waist and pale skin. Her finely brushed ginger hair glittered with the gold spray she'd used earlier that evening. Edward, underneath his jacket, had just decided to wear a plain white shirt, leaving two top buttons undone. The pair danced flawlessly, completely oblivious to the others dancing around them.

"*Who* is *that*?" Rose's mother spat as she looked Charlotte up and down with disgust.

The Calvert family, except Rose, all stood and watched horrified as the prince danced with the human girl. Rose's father looked at Rose with anger and frustration. *What have you been doing all this time?*

"I did everything you instructed," Rose replied, not even bothering to look at her father. "He's just not interested."

Dominic McKnight watched intently as Rose's father began horribly lecturing her on her failure to snare Nicholas. Roses' facial features didn't even flinch and he waved an angry fist in front of her face. Dominic watched with dark narrow eyes for a few more minutes, but eventually excusing himself from his mother, father and older brother, Dominic briskly walked over to the Calvert family. Politely, he bowed his head in respect. "Mr Calvert," he said, earning an annoyed looked from older, finely dressed man. "I was wondering, do I have permission to dance with Rose?"

Mrs Calvert, a small, woman with bob cut hair, sneered in disgust while Mr Calvert looked horrified. "No," was his simple reply. "Rose will dance with no one but Nicholas."

"Well, as you can see, Nicholas is already dancing with a lady. And, most likely, has no intention of dancing with anyone else. So rather, than waste your lovely daughter, I'm sure—"

"I *said no*."

Dominic's eyes narrowed dangerously. He took a step forward so that he was only inches away from Mr Calvert's face. Rose, her mother, and younger sister watched in astonishment as Dominic's already large figure, seemed to tower over Mr Calvert. "This is the last time I will ask you politely, sir," he practically growled. "Rose may be your daughter, but she is *not* your meal ticket. So, you will start treating her with a bit more respect. You are not a Lord. *You* have *no* power here." Mr Calvert didn't know what to say. Even as Dominic took Rose by the hand and led her away, he, his wife, and youngest daughter remained speechless.

"Thank you." Rose whispered as Dominic led the dance, her copper orange dress sweeping against the floor.

Gazing down at her, Dominic smiled and nodded. "You look stunning tonight."

Rose couldn't hide her grateful smile. Even as Dominic twisted her into a twirl, the smile glowed brighter than the chandelier above. However, the dance didn't last very long, as the music had stopped. All heads turned to look at the front of the foyer, where a woman in red stood.

Chapter Thirteen

Nicholas let go of Charlotte's waist, and calmly walked over to the woman who had just floated into the Rinaldi's foyer. Charlotte watched with curiosity as the pair seemed to exchange words, a little laughter and smiles. The woman, Charlotte had to admit, was stunning. Her hair was long, dark ruby red and curly. Her eyes, were like emeralds. And her ball gown, was almost as red as her hair. The dress was complimented by a gold, diamond, and pearl choker. The woman, to Charlotte's surprise, took a slight step back to bow her head and while lifting her dress, did a curtsy.

Nicholas then held out his hand and led the woman to the centre, making everyone part like the red sea. Taking their positions, Nicholas waved for the music to start again, and the couple danced. Charlotte awkwardly took a step back to join the crowd, who were all watching intently. After a few minutes of just Nicholas dancing with the mysterious woman, a few others began to join in. Once again, the room became like the coral reef, a magical swirl of colour.

Biting her lip awkwardly, Charlotte politely pushed her way through the crowd and back up the stairs. From the top floor, she folded her arms over the bannister and just watched silently. Feeling just a little sad and disappointed, Charlotte couldn't help but frown as Nicholas then led the woman over to Elise, who smiled broadly while pecking the woman's cheek. The three became engaged in conversation.

"Beautiful, isn't she?"

Charlotte turned her head to the side to see a very large, muscular man with a black moustache and finely trimmed goatee, standing next to her. Like all the other guests, he was wearing a dinner jacket. Charlotte stood straight and cleared her throat. "Yes," she breathed quietly, looking back down at the woman. "Very beautiful."

"I don't believe we've been introduced," the man continued in a bold, confident voice. "I'm William Rinaldi, Nicholas's father."

Charlotte practically jumped to stand up straight. Quickly straightening her dress and tucking her hair behind her ear, she held out her hand. "No, I'm sorry. We haven't. I'm C-Charlotte, Charlotte—"

"Davenport," William said quickly, his moustache lifting with a small smile as he shook her hand. "You're Carl's niece. And I've heard a lot about you from Nicholas."

"All good, I hope?"

William didn't answer, he just looked back down at Nicholas and the woman. Charlotte noticed how much Nicholas looked like his father. The same jet black hair, same jet black eyes. Only, this man was taller, more muscular and certainly had a more fearsome and intimidating aura around him. "That's Mina Cross," he said, nodding down at the woman in the red ball gown. "She's been a good friend of Nicholas's since the day they were born."

"They're just friends then?" Charlotte muttered.

"For now. I'm hoping the boy will see sense and settle with Mina after he's finished college," William said simply, carefully watching Nicholas from above. He then glanced at Charlotte who seemed to have gone rigid. Putting a large hand on her shoulder, William slowly turned Charlotte so she was completely facing him. "Charlotte," he started. "Why are you here?"

Charlotte looked at him with a little surprise, then she shrugged. "I don't know. Because Nicholas invited me? I guess."

"And you came? Just like that?"

"Well, yeah. Nicholas has been a good friend to me so far, so—"

"*Just* a friend?"

Charlotte just simply nodded, but William's eyes studied her closely. Releasing her shoulder, his size seemed to increase. "Look," he started in a low, serious voice. "I don't know what my son has told you, or what he said to make you come to my house. Or whether you're just after his money. But whatever it is, it stops now. You…you are just not suitable for him."

Charlotte stared in utter shock up at the sleek haired man. Swallowing the lump in her throat, she tried to muster up the courage to speak. But William's words, had stung her like a bee. "But…he…he said I was important, in class he—"

"There are many people around Nicholas who he claims to be important. It doesn't mean they're important to *him* for any particular reason. The maids that clean this house are important to him. It doesn't mean he has a romantic interest."

Charlotte's lip trembled as the heat rose to her eyes. Her vision blurred with tears as she gingerly touched her lips. "We kissed."

"He's a college student," William stated softly. "What do you expect? You won't be the only one."

Charlotte just stood silent for a moment, then she looked back down at Nicholas and Mina. They both looked so happy in their conversation, so content, so comfortable, so *right* for each other. Even Elise seemed so much happier and comfortable to be around Mina, more than when she was around Charlotte. Nicholas had forgotten Charlotte as soon as Mina had walked through the door. For the first time, Charlotte had let her guard down.

"I'll tell your uncle that you're leaving," William stated as he walked past Charlotte.

Charlotte didn't even have time to respond, she just stared at the spot where William had stood. Then she just gathered her dress, and ran to her room. Slamming the bedroom door behind her, Charlotte pressed her back against it and looked up to the ceiling. The tears were flowing freely now, and Charlotte couldn't hold it in anymore. Never in her life had she ever been told she wasn't good enough; and William's words echoed in her head. *You are just not suitable for him.* Crying uncontrollably, Charlotte slid to the floor and put her head in her hands. The magenta dress that Nicholas had given her, ruffled at her feet. Her entire body shook as she wept.

She didn't know how long she'd sat on the floor crying, when a shuffle in the room made her stop. Charlotte lifted her head, and wiped the water from her face, and looked towards the window. Her blurry brown eyes narrowed curiously in the dark. In the dim light, she could make out a small silhouette of a child who stood at the edge of her room. A little boy, wearing a tiny dinner suit, with strangely bright green eyes. Obviously, the boy was from the party downstairs, but how did he get into Charlotte's room?

"Hello?" Charlotte sniffed.

"Hello?" The little boy echoed innocently.

"Are you alright?" Charlotte asked as she stood up, wiping her face. "Are you lost?"

The little boy just stood still and started to play innocently with his jacket. "I'm looking for someone."

"Who?"

The little boy just giggled; he waved Charlotte eagerly to come closer. Charlotte sighed, she wasn't in the mood for games, but she obliged. She walked over, and the little boy took her slender hand in his tiny one, gently pulling her down to his level. Now kneeling, Charlotte was almost eye level with the little boy. He was cute, with a chubby face, a tiny mop of light brown hair and gentle baby blue eyes that hand a hint of green. Charlotte could have sworn that they were glowing. The little boy waved Charlotte to lean in closer so that her ear was practically touching his face. "My master told me to bring someone back to him." He whispered.

"Oh really?" Charlotte whispered back, smiling slightly in amusement at the boy's game. "Who?"

"You."

Charlotte frowned with confusion. "What?" she looked up, and immediately jumped back in utter horror. The little boy's face twisted into a horrible, distorted mess, his once tiny little teeth protruding his bottom lip. His innocent eyes had become dilated, enraged, and they *were* glowing! Charlotte scrambled to her feet, her dress tangling around her ankles as she ran towards the door. In a rage, the boy pounced to an incredible height, and rugby tackled Charlotte back to the floor, snapping and shrieking like a rabid dog. His teeth, long and sharp and only inches away from Charlotte's face. Like a starved animal, saliva violently began to froth from his mouth as desperation started kicking in. Charlotte punched the boy in the head a number of times as she tried desperately to fight him off. They rolled around the room, banging so hard into the bed, the wardrobe and the dressing table that the room shook like an earthquake. The chair fell on top of them both which the boy immediately reduced to splinters. Then, with a sickening grin and a tilt of his head, the boy got strange iron grip of Charlotte's wrist, and bit down. *Hard.* The pain was excruciating and burned like fire. Blood immediately poured through the penetrated skin. Wide eyed, in agony and in horror, Charlotte could do nothing but shriek.

"*Help me!*"

Chapter Fourteen

The bedroom door burst open and the boy screeched in fury, like a baboon, at being discovered. He jumped off Charlotte to grip one of the posts of the bed. His little face smeared with blood and frothy foam. Charlotte held her burning, red dripping wrist delicately as she dazedly tilted her head to look at the bedroom door. Her heart stopped.

"Oh no…" she breathed.

Standing in the doorway were Nicholas, Dominic, Edward, Rose and Bianca. They were hissing like wolves, their features were twisted with snarls. Charlotte shook in horror at the size of their teeth, which had grown to an extraordinary length and sharpness. Their eyes were practically glowing green in the dark. The sounds that were coming from their throats were out of this world, completely unrecognisable. All of them were completely focused on the boy, and Nicholas was the first one to pounce into the air. Charlotte screamed and covered her face as he collided with the bedpost, slashing as he tried to grab the boy. However, the boy managed to avoid Nicholas's slashing hands as he pounced into the air. Edward grabbed the boy by the ankle mid-air and pulled him straight down with hard, bone crunching thud. Both, he and Dominic cornered the boy by the wardrobe, easing themselves closer to him, but at the same time trying to not let him get past. The boy glared and snarled at each of them, slashing his little hands, his glowing eyes darting from one to the other; they responded with their own roars and barks.

Both Bianca and Rose rushed straight to Charlotte who was still shaking and bleeding on the floor. "Let me see," Rose said gently, trying not to show her teeth. She carefully took Charlotte's wrist. The puncture wounds were deep and raw. "Bianca," she said finally. "Go see if you can get warm water and bandages. Hurry!"

Before Bianca could respond, the boy flew towards her and knocked her into the wall with a hard thud. Now, they were scrapping like lions. The pair flew across the room and crashed into the dressing table, smashing it to pieces. Bianca jumped elegantly up from the rubble. A tiny trickle of blood escaped the corner of her mouth. Licking the blood away, Bianca inspected the rip in her royal blue dress. Her glassy glowing eyes glared daggers at the boy as he stood from the remains of the dressing table. "You're getting annoying," she hissed.

Before the boy could stand up straight, Bianca dived forward. Landing palm first onto the floor, putting all her weight onto her wrist, she twisted her body and kicked the boy straight into Dominic's arms. Dominic caught the boy into a headlock. While he was screeching and snapping, trying to bite his arm, Dominic gripped the boy's head and with an annoyed growl, twisted.

Charlotte cringed at the sound of the boy's neck snapping. She stared, horrified, as Dominic dropped the limp boy to the shredded, blood stained carpet. Bianca ran out of the room with lightning speed and Nicholas was at Charlotte's side, cradling her like a baby. His animalistic features had almost returned to normal.

Elise and William bolted into the room, their eyes darting all over. They observed the shredded chair, shattered dressing table, and scent and sight of blood all over the carpet. With the light flooding in from the hallway, all glowing green eyes returned back to their natural colours. "*What* on earth is going on in *my* house?" William growled.

"Charlotte was attacked," Nicholas responded, not even looking up at his father, "by *that* thing."

"Oh my God!" Elise said in shock as she picked up her dress and rushed to Charlotte's side.

William looked down at Dominic's feet, his face twisted. "Is it dead?"

"No, my Lord," Dominic replied. "Just stunned."

"Well then," William responded through gritted teeth, "would you be so kind as to finish it, and remove it from my house?"

Dominic nodded and scooped the boy up, and carried him out of the room just as Bianca rushed in with water and bandages. Charlotte's uncle Carl followed, closely behind. He was dripping with sweat and his blue eyes were wide and bulging from their sockets. His chest heaved heavily as he knelt down next to Charlotte, gasping in horror at her unsightly wrist. "Oh my God..." He breathed, running his hand through his hair.

Charlotte was still trembling with fear in Nicholas's arms. Elise and Rose had cleaned as much of the wounds as possible and had tried to bandage them as gently. As soon as Charlotte saw her uncle, her half-closed eyes opened a little wider. "V-vampires," she stuttered. "I-it was a v-vampire, they're a-all v-vampires, all—"

Carl put a finger to his niece's lips and hushed her gently. "Don't speak."

Charlotte's bottom lip trembled, slowly, she looked around. William stood in the doorway, Elise and Rose knelt by her side, Nicholas was cradling her, Edward and Bianca sat on the window seat. Looking back at her uncle, a tear slid down her cheek. "You knew," she said shakily.

When Carl didn't say anything or even blink, Charlotte realised it was true. Her lips trembled, and she sat silently for a moment. Nicholas pulled her closer to him protectively. Looking at Carl, he quietly asked. "Did you search the grounds?"

"Yes, the Seekers are searching everywhere now as we speak."

William's frame towered over them, he glared straight at Charlotte. "I want her *out* of my house."

"What?" Carl said, shocked as he looked up at William. "After what she's just been through?"

"I will not have your family destroy mine any further!"

"She needs time to rest! She's been bitten. She just—"

"Out!"

Elise stood up straight and glared, appalled at her husband. "Oh, William for goodness sake!"

"*I said I want her out*!"

"Charlotte stays."

All eyes fell on Nicholas. William's face dropped slightly. "What?"

Nicholas didn't flinch, instead, he looked up defiantly into his father's eye. "If Charlotte leaves, I will go with her."

William hissed angrily through gritted teeth. "*What?*"

"Charlotte needs protecting, and you know it. This is the safest place for her. If you make her leave, you're going to risk everyone's lives. You heard what the committee said in the meeting. However, if you insist on having another blood bath, by all means, let her go. But *I* will be going with her."

William's teeth grinded, and his fists clenched in anger at his son's defiance. "You're forgetting who you're talking to, boy."

All eyes were on William now. Either waiting for a verbal response, or for him to strike Nicholas. William's beady black eyes became sharp slits, like a snake. He looked at Charlotte who was silent, pale and absolutely exhausted in Nicholas's arms. Then, he looked at his wife, whose clear peppermint eyes, dared him to say another word. Growling, William turned and left the room.

Elise then looked down at Nicholas. "So," she said softly. "You do care for her?" When Nicholas didn't respond, Elise then looked down at Charlotte with a little concern. "You'd better get her to another room. She's had a nasty shock."

As though she was a valuable glass piece, Nicholas carefully lifted Charlotte from the floor. As he carried her silently out of the room, she wrapped her arms around his neck, and buried her head into his chest. Feeling her tears soaking into his shirt, Nicholas paused, and turned to look at Carl.

"Carl," he said. "She knows."

Carl didn't respond, he just bowed his head, and stared at the blood stained patch where Charlotte had been laying. Nicolas turned and carried Charlotte out of the room.

Chapter Fifteen

After getting her undressed and cleaned, Nicholas tucked Charlotte into bed. "Are you alright?" he asked gently. Charlotte simply responded with a 'are you serious?' look. Nicholas just nodded and thinned his lips. "Silly question."

Charlotte sat up in bed; her stained purple dress had been tossed to the floor, and the small diamond pins had been removed, allowing her dark chocolate hair to flow down her back. While Nicholas had been trying to discreetly undress her and clean her, Charlotte had remained silent and pale. As she stared down at her bandaged wrist, with a solemn crease of her brow, she looked at Nicholas. "What are you?"

Nicholas sighed; he ran a hand through his ebony hair. "There have been many names, to be honest," he started. "Demons, blood suckers, the undead, the cold ones, servants of the devil" – Nicholas paused for a moment – "but we're commonly known as vampires."

"How long have you been…?"

"Since birth. I was born this way."

"Your mum and dad, they're vampires too?"

"Yes."

"And, all those people at the party, they're…?"

"Yes."

"Do you live forever?"

"Yes."

Charlotte gulped. "Are you…do you kill—"

"Humans? No. We feed on animals. Well, I don't; the rest of my kind do," Nicholas said simply. "Apart from my father and Mina."

"I don't understand." Charlotte said, her frown deepening.

"There are different kinds of vampires. Vampires, as you know them, then there's me, my father and Mina, who are known simply as rare bloods; then, there's Rogues." Nicholas paused as the words sank in. "Rare bloods, are vampires that do not need to feed for a *very* long time. Months can go by and we won't feel any different. Unlike the rest of my kind who need to feed on a regular basis. Then, there's Rogues. To our kind, this is the most dangerous and lowest of our species. Sometimes they're mindless killing machines, sometimes they're very much in control. They are the ones that won't hesitate to kill a human; even a child if they're hungry enough."

Charlotte glanced down at her wrist. "Then, that boy, he…"

"He wasn't a Rogue," Nicholas said, his lips thinning. "To be honest, I don't really know what he was or why he was here. Or *how* he even got past the Seekers."

Charlotte's face fell as she quickly remembered what the boy had said before attacking her. "He said," Charlotte started, "that his master had sent him to take *me* back. At first, I thought it was a game, and then…" Charlotte trailed off as she looked back down at her wrist. Nicholas frowned and his black eyes narrowed as he quickly remembered the old man in the park. *Master? Fake Prince?* It was all starting to make sense.

Charlotte then looked back up at Nicholas. "What's a Seeker?"

"Seekers? They've been around for as long as we have. They're part of a secret organisation known as the Seeker Association. They're vampire hunters *and* protectors. At first, they despised our kind, did everything they could to wipe us out, and vice versa. But then, both sides began to get tired of a war that just didn't seem to end. So, they decided to work together. My family hired them to help hunt down rogues that threatened the peace, and the seekers got well-paid work, and got the chance to protect the rest of the humankind. It was agreed that vampires could live in peace alongside humans as long as we didn't harm them, unless absolutely necessary."

"And," Charlotte began, "my uncle, he's part of this organisation?" Nicholas gave a simple, slow nod. Charlotte leaned back into her pillow in disbelief. "Why didn't he tell me?"

"To protect you," Carl said from the bedroom door, making both Nicholas and Charlotte look up. Charlotte noticed he had taken his coat and stab vest off; even from the bed, she could see the tired dark circles under his eyes. Carl smiled softly at Charlotte, then looked sternly at Nicholas. "Please, if you don't mind?"

"Of course." Nicholas replied as he stood from the bed, but not before kissing Charlotte on the forehead. Passing Carl, he didn't say a word, and closed the door behind him.

Carl made his way to the four-poster bed to sit next to Charlotte. He ran a hand soothingly through her dark hair. "How you feeling, kiddo?"

"Seriously?" Charlotte snapped, anger filling her eyes. "So far tonight, I've been bitten by Eddie Munster, found out that vampires exist, and on top of that, I found out that my uncle is like bloody Batman. Other than that, I'm just peachy!"

"Oh good," Carl replied, wide eyed. "Glad to see you're taking it well."

Charlotte glared at him. "Why didn't you just tell me the truth?"

"Because I didn't want to involve you with *any* of this," Carl responded with a sigh. "I didn't want you to be involved with the association, with the Rinaldis, with vampires. That's why I didn't want you going near them. I didn't want you to go down the same road as your parents. I didn't want you—"

"Whoa, whoa," Charlotte interrupted, palm facing Carl. "My parents *died* in a car accident, when I was a baby," Charlotte stated confidently, but Carl's shifty reaction told her otherwise. "Oh, fantastic," she hissed, folding her arms.

"Charlotte," Carl said in a begging voice, his blue eyes pleading with her not to be angry. "Your mum and dad loved you so much, *so much* that they made me promise not to tell you. They didn't want to involve you in any of this. They wanted you to have a normal life, *not* as a hunter. After they married and had you, they were planning on giving up the organisation and handing it to someone else. But then, they—"

"They *what*?" Charlotte snapped angrily. "Abandoned me?"

Carl's face fell. "No," he said in a low voice. "They were murdered by a Rogue, by James Rinaldi."

Charlotte's heart sank as her eyes widened. "James? As in Nicholas's older brother?"

Carl nodded. "James was furious with your mother that she had chosen the chief of the association, your father, over him. You see, Rachel had been chosen by James, Elise, and William as the perfect woman to unite the association with the vampires. Rachel was well-respected amongst everyone, fearless and loving too. James became besotted with her. But Rachel just didn't feel the same way. She married Matthew instead. Everyone else seemed understanding, everyone except James. Shortly after you were born, James began going on a rampage, killing humans, attacking members of the association. Rachel and Matthew stood against him, but he was too strong. After that, it was Nicholas who eventually took him down. And it was William who decided to lock James away." Carl paused. "Absolutely broke his heart, locking his own son away. But William knew, if he didn't, James would wipe everything out without a second thought. Since then, William has never trusted our family."

"Locked him away?" Charlotte said with confusion. "You said he just disappeared!"

"After he turned, he may as well have been dead."

Charlotte listened with disbelief and astonishment. Well, at least all this explained William's cold attitude towards her and why he wanted her out of the house. But, Charlotte genuinely didn't know what to make of all this; surely she was dreaming and would wake up. But the tightness in her chest, told her otherwise. "Those girls," she breathed. "Lucy, Casey, Sam, Louisa. They weren't killed by anything human, were they?"

"We believe it was done by a Rogue. We've been trying to hunt it down but it's grown to be quick and strong." Carl paused again. "We believe it's James."

"James?" Charlotte repeated. "But he's locked away, isn't he?"

"He *was*," Carl said. "He managed to escape, though we have no idea how. Since he got out, there have been some very unusual deaths to young girls, all with unusual injuries. No human can break bones into splinters. Another reason why we think it's James, is because all the girls that were killed, all resemble Elise. There was a massive meeting about it."

A shiver ran up Charlotte's spine. "Well, what does he want? Just to kill girls who look like Elise?"

"We think he's building up for something else. Something bigger," Carl replied. Then, he looked at Charlotte with worry in his eyes. "We think he's after you."

"*Me*?" Charlotte squeaked, looking at him wide eyed. "Why *me*?"

"He couldn't have the mother so now he wants the daughter. And if he gets you, he'll have control of the Seekers Association. And if that happens, he could order a mass murder of *everyone* who crossed him, and possibly bring the association down to its knees. Think about it, all the girls were killed near your area. Why else hasn't he moved on?"

"What's it got to do with me?"

"With your mum and dad gone, you being too young, it was my responsibility to run the organisation until you were ready. Matthew was the first born, so he was the chief, you are his daughter, therefore you are the next chief. But, your mum and dad did not want that. So, we all promised them that you would not takeover. But, I have to admit, with things being the way they are…" Carl then paused and put a hand on Charlotte's shoulder. "Charlotte, it's been agreed by, well, *everyone,* that you should start learning a bit of self-defence with us. I promised your mum and dad I wouldn't tell you anything, but with the attack last night, you've become a target. Someone knows you're here. That's why, when you told me Nicholas had asked to meet you, I didn't like it. A Rinaldi Princess will not be welcomed as the Chief of—"

"*Princess?*" Charlotte squeaked in a high voice. "What are you talking about?"

"You heard Nicholas in the other room. He admitted it out loud! He's got no intention of letting you out of his sight. That means he's already decided on who will be the next queen. Should William and Elise ever give it up that is."

"Wait, wait, wait," Charlotte said in a rush. "*You're* telling *me*, that Nicholas wants me to become a vampire so that he can marry me? And if I do, I'll become queen?"

"That's exactly what I'm saying to you. William is the king, Elise is the queen, Nicholas is the prince, and, if you accept, *you* will be the princess. And if you and Nicholas do join in matrimony that means in one way or another, he will have some control over the association."

"But you just said that a Chief cannot be a Rinaldi Princess?"

"I said you wouldn't be welcome, *not* that it wasn't possible."

"How…wait, what? How can they be royalty? They don't live at Buckingham Palace!"

"The Rinaldi's are the only family to have the longest rare gene in their bloodline. Therefore, in their world, they are the royals. *Everyone* wants a piece of them. To be able to live without an urge to feed, is a very rare gift for vampires. But it's not something that you can get at will. Nicholas inherited the gene from William, but James didn't."

"What about that Mina Cross? William said he wanted Nicholas to marry *her*."

"Mina also has a rare gene. But hers came about more recently, therefore she does not have a status as high as the Rinaldis. And let's face it, Nicholas won't marry anyone he doesn't class as suitable. They're just friends. Mina is the last of her family with the gene, but she will never be classed as royalty by others. Even though she is William's favourite."

Charlotte put her head in her hands and groaned. "This is getting to be a very strange weekend."

Carl leaned over and landed a small kiss on the top of her dark hair. "I know it's going to be hard, but try and get some sleep." Charlotte just groaned and nodded at the same time as Carl silently left the room.

Chapter Sixteen

The next morning was grey, bleak and dreary. Tiny droplets of rain gently patted the Georgian style window of the sitting room.

William Rinaldi sat silently in the red velvet armchair, staring in deep thought into the flames of the open fire. After the incident upstairs from the night before, this is where he had come. Just for a bit of peace and quiet. But the maid was silently fluttering around the room, dusting every inch she could reach.

The sitting room door opened, and Elise walked into the room, marched straight over, stood in front of William, and sternly folded her arms. Judging by her damp and windswept appearance, Elise had just come back from a run, and a hunt. The smell of rabbit wafted towards William. Sensing an argument, the maid quickly gathered her cleaning equipment and scurried silently out of the room.

"So," Elise started, as the maid fully closed the door. "You're just going to sit and sulk in here all day?" William just grunted. Elise sighed and took a seat in the armchair opposite. "You can't blame Charlotte for what happened," she said softly. "What happened to our son was awful. But it happened, and there is no one in this whole world who is to blame. Rogues are a risk that *all* of our kind faces. No matter what their status is."

William didn't even blink. "I don't blame Charlotte."

"Oh?" Elise responded with surprise as she leaned back into her chair. "You certainly seemed to last night."

"I'm angry," William replied with a clenched jaw. "Angry at that family, angry at Rachel, angry at the association, angry with…with myself. We all missed the signs." William's face dropped slightly. "And now Nicholas is going the same way."

"Nicholas will do what he believes is right," Elise replied softly, but firmly. "If he truly cares about Charlotte, he will stand by her no matter what. You can't treat him coldly for following what *we* have always told him to do. Just because he has fallen for a human, a Davenport, does not mean he is any less our son."

"Humans," William sneered. "More trouble than what they're worth."

Elise's eyes dropped slightly. "*I*," she said in a low voice, "was also one of those humans."

William turned his head to look at his wife, whose eyes had flicked back up to look him straight in the eye. "You were different."

"How was I different from the others? Because I was chosen by the king?" William rubbed his forehead, exasperated, as an awkward silence filled the room. After a few moments, Elise leaned forward. "I lost James too. I gave birth to him, and it was painful. But it was *nothing,* compared to the pain of losing him. But now, he's gone. Our son, is no longer the son we raised" – Elise gulped back the tears – "and he does have to be stopped, by any means necessary."

William stared for a moment as his wife's words echoed in his mind. It had killed her to say them. She had been sitting in the meetings with the Seeker Association alongside William, and listened to every word. And now, Elise had given her first-born son, the death sentence. William leaned forward and took her slender hand in is. "I'm sorry," he said. "I was just so angry that I forgot that you were suffering too. I'm terrified, Elise. Terrified that we're going to lose Nicholas too."

Elise took her husband's face in her hands. "We won't. Nicholas is not James. He is strong, and so is Charlotte. People may not realise it yet, but she is very much like Rachel."

William slowly nodded, then looked back into the open fire. "That's what worries me."

"Rose?" Nicholas said, a little surprised to see the blonde haired girl standing in the hallway, outside Charlotte's door. "Are you alright?"

Rose nodded sheepishly. "Yes, I am, thank you."

Nicholas arched an eyebrow. "Can I help you with something?"

"No, my Lord," Rose replied quietly. "It's more, what I can do for you."

Nicholas's face fell. "Rose, you're a lovely girl and any man would be lucky to have you. But, I can't do it anymore. I have Charlotte to—"

"No," Rose interrupted, shaking her head. "It's not that. That's not why I'm here." She paused as Nicholas frowned with curiosity. "I came to…I came to apologise. And to tell you that, whatever has happened between us, I'm still…I'm still loyal to you, and your family."

Nicholas was shocked. "Why are you apologising?"

"For my behaviour before. Last night, what happened to Charlotte, I saw a change in you. I didn't realise you felt so strongly. I didn't even have feelings for you when we first started going to college" – Rose paused to take a shaky breath – "but then I did. But you see, in the beginning, I was just doing what my family…" Rose trailed off. "Anyway, I apologise. To you, and to Charlotte."

Nicholas stood in the doorway, feeling a little puzzled. Thinking deeply about what she had said, he smiled and put a cool hand on her slender shoulder. "Rose, you don't need to apologise to me. I know how ambitious your family is, and what they told you to do. You deserve so much more than what they say. You've been a very good friend to me. And loyal. And that's why" – he paused a moment, allowing his smile to broaden – "I trust you completely, Rose. With my life, and with Charlotte's."

Rose looked up in astonishment, her glassy hazel eyes, shimmering like jewels. Her mouth was slightly agape. This was not expected. Rose had expected a cold dismissal; to be told never to darken Nicholas's door again. But this was a genuine comfort that she was still welcomed as a friend by him. Looking into his dark ebony eyes, Rose then bowed her head, allowing her thick wavy locks to fall. She couldn't hide the appreciative smile. "Thank you, for saying that."

Chapter Seventeen

As the sun set around the Rinaldi home, the sky became a warm mixture of gold and pink around the house. It almost looked like a pastel drawing. Bianca and Edward watched Charlotte like hawks as she walked around the garden. It was the first time she'd stepped outside since she had arrived at the Rinaldi home. Charlotte was a little nervous about walking around on her own, knowing what they were. So, as they passed each other, Charlotte had tried to start a little conversation, and Edward and Bianca had agreed politely with everything she said. But that didn't seem to ease the awkwardness. Charlotte just politely excused herself and quickly walked over to the apple blossom trees. The pair just continued to watch her from the fountain.

"She doesn't trust us," Bianca said, smirking.

"Would you? We did give her a bit of a scare," Edward replied, also smirking.

"I still can't believe it," Bianca said, linking Edward's arm. "She's the next chief to be."

"I told you, Nicholas wanted her for a reason."

"You think he wants her for the association?"

"Oh, without a doubt," Edward replied with amusement. "But, I do also believe he does care for her, in a small way. Otherwise, he wouldn't have stood up to William."

"That was a brave thing to do, I have to admit," Bianca replied as she perched on the edge of the fountain. "We'll see what she's made of. Although, some won't accept her."

"That's true," Edward agreed, watching Charlotte from across the garden as she picked at the apple blossom. "She will be tested."

"One thing I don't understand, if Nicholas wants to control the Seekers, why didn't he just try and take it?"

"If you were a human, would you take orders from the very thing you hunted? And vice versa. Would you take orders from a human?"

"I see your point," Bianca replied with a nod.

"And also," Edward continued, "when you take something, you can spend your entire life fighting to keep it."

Bianca just sighed as she looked up at the pastel sky. "It's a beautiful evening."

Edward looked up and after a moment, nodded in agreement. Then, looked at Bianca. His seaweed green eyes admired her for a moment. "It is." Bianca looked at him, and smiled. The sky was getting darker and that familiar heated tingling in her body began. Edward must have sensed it as he held out his hand to assist her from the fountain's edge. Together, at lightning speed, they both disappeared into the apple blossom trees.

Meanwhile, Charlotte snapped a branch from one of the trees to take a small clump of pink apple blossom in her hands. She gently ran her fingertips over the soft petals; thinking about the warning Nicholas had angrily given her earlier that evening.

"When this gets out, some are going to come after you. And not just scary little boys. You have nothing to defend yourself with. I'm simply asking you stay with me. The end of the year is coming and you're running out of time. I don't care if you like me or not. There are spies everywhere. Let me help you, and I'll keep you safe."

It was an ultimatum. Charlotte had felt so overwhelmed, that she couldn't bring herself to answer Nicholas straight away. Nicholas seemed angry at first, but then he became slightly more understanding. If Charlotte did want this life, she would live it with Nicholas. And Charlotte, as it had become all too clear, was far too valuable to give up. However, as tempting as a royal life was, Charlotte couldn't help but think because of vampires, her parents were dead. Because of vampires, she'd been bitten. Because of vampires, four innocent girls were dead. And then, there was the Seekers Association. It was too much. Charlotte looked around the garden, at the trees, the grass, the driveway, the fountain, the house. It was *all* too much. Charlotte sighed sadly as she dropped the petals, watching as they flittered to ground. The sun had set and the air had become colder. The lights shining through the Georgian windows of the house were lit like a lighthouse on the cliffs, offering warmth and protection. But Charlotte didn't want any part of it. She wanted to go home.

Charlotte walked back to the house, rubbing her arms. Quietly, she walked up the steps, and opened the front door, trying not to disturb the rest of the house. Smiling sadly at the bright and beautiful décor, she made her way up the mahogany stairs and straight to her room. Opening the door, Charlotte flicked on the light, and stopped. Nicholas was sitting on her window seat, looking solemnly out the bedroom window, with one leg casually hanging off the edge. With his black V-necked shirt and leather jacket, he looked like a model. Charlotte wet her lips, and stepped into the room, closing the door behind her.

"I need to tell you something," Charlotte said simply, bowing her head. "I thought about what you said, and I've decided." She paused as she felt tears fill her eyes. "I can't do it. I'm sorry, there's too much involved. I just…I can't give up my life to do something that I just learned about five minutes ago. It's all too much. I'm so confused at the moment. I know you said you needed an answer, and maybe after college or when I've had more time…" Charlotte paused to take a shaky breath as the tears rolled down her cheeks. "I'm sorry, Nicholas."

Nicholas, for what seemed forever, did not move. But then his lips seemed to curl into, from what Charlotte could make out, a smirk. Nicholas slid off the window seat, and walked silently and confidently towards her. To Charlotte's surprise, he wrapped his arms around her. Charlotte couldn't help but close her eyes and rest her head on his shoulder. And that's how they stood. But then, Nicholas began to smell her hair, making Charlotte feel a little uneasy. She tried to gently pull away, but Nicholas squeezed her, just a little too tight. "Nicholas" – she breathed with discomfort – "you're hurting me." It shocked her even more when Nicholas buried his head in the crook of her neck, and licked it.

"Am I hurting you as much as that little boy?" he purred into her neck. "I told him not to be too rough with you."

That voice? Charlotte immediately pulled herself out of the intruder's grip, however he kept a firm hold of her wrist. Shaking, Charlotte stared wide eyed, in horror. Instead of black eyes, his eyes were green. "You…you're not Nicholas!"

The intruders smirk widened. "No. But call me James."

Nicholas was the first one to bolt out of the room. Running straight up the stairs and to the end of the hallway. He sensed it. Nicholas kicked open Charlotte's door, and froze.

In the open window, Charlotte was being held unconscious by a tall, black haired, green eyed, intruder. Against her beige, creamy skin the pair of red raw dots was unsightly. Nicholas immediately felt his fury rise within him; unable to hold it back, he bared his full-grown teeth, and with a snarl, he roared.

"*James*!"

James just stood silent, and smirked. Then with a sneering laugh and a flash of lightening, James, and Charlotte were gone.